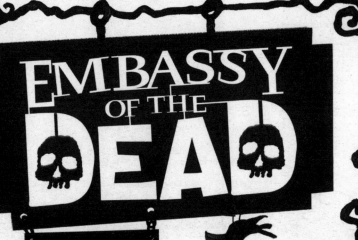

EMBASSY OF THE DEAD

HANGMAN'S CROSSING

Will Mabbitt

With illustrations by

Chris Mould

Orion
Children's Books

ORION CHILDREN'S BOOKS

First published in Great Britain in 2019 by Hodder and Stoughton

1 3 5 7 9 10 8 6 4 2

Text copyright © Will Mabbitt, 2019
Illustrations copyright © Chris Mould, 2019

The moral rights of the author and illustrator have been asserted.

A CIP catalogue record for this book
is available from the British Library.

ISBN 978-1-5101-0457-0

Printed and bound in Great Britain by Clays Ltd, Elcograf S.p.A.

The paper and board used in this book are made
from wood from responsible sources.

MIX
Paper from
responsible sources
FSC® C104740
FSC
www.fsc.org

Orion Children's Books
An imprint of
Hachette Children's Group
Part of Hodder and Stoughton
Carmelite House
50 Victoria Embankment
London EC4Y 0DZ

An Hachette UK Company
www.hachette.co.uk www.hachettechildrens.co.uk

For Thomas

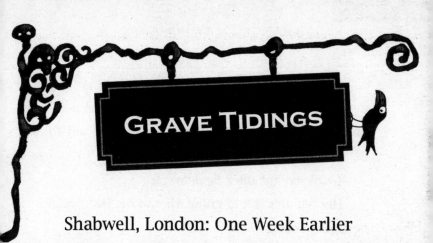

GRAVE TIDINGS

Shabwell, London: One Week Earlier

G hosts don't feel the cold.

All the same, Amber Chase lifted the collar of her flying jacket to protect herself from the freezing night air. She'd been dead for ninety years, but old habits die hard.

Unusually for the city, the snow was beginning to settle. A light coating covered the dead-end street, a thin blanket of white concealing the grime beneath.

Amber kept to the shadows. With darkness came safety. Even though she was invisible to the vast majority of the living, it was best to take precautions.

Besides, *it wasn't the living she was afraid of.*

Something bad was crossing over. Something worse than she'd ever expected. She had a time, a date, and now ... a name. For the sake of the here-and-now and the happy-ever-Afterworld, it had to be stopped.

Grave tidings must be delivered.

Her handler would know what to do. He should be here by now.

Where was he?

Her eyes scanned the high brick walls of the alley. She was looking for the triple-crossed logo of the Embassy. A sign that would show he was here, somewhere, waiting in the shadows.

But she was at the dead end now and there was no symbol. She looked to the night sky, cursing her rashness – the trait that had got her killed in the first place.

Ninety years gone by and she could still smell her mistake: the acrid burning scent of her plane's over-heated engine. She could still hear the altimeter ticking down.

800 feet. 700 feet. 500 feet. 200 feet ...

A countdown to the impact of the rocky desert that was hurtling towards her. A different pilot would have settled for breaking the world distance record. But not her. She had to push the plane to its limits . . .

The only part of the plane they'd found was a small piece of metal bearing the words she'd carefully painted on the plane's fuselage: *Against all odds.*

She blinked away the memory of her death. Something had caught her eye.

Back down the alley a shadow peeled away from the wall. A creeping puddle of darkness that merged and grew upwards from the snow until it formed a jagged, faintly humanoid shape, faceless and grey, flickering into solidity as it paused to sniff the air.

Another shape peeled from the wall. Then one more. Now there were three creatures in total.

They must have known she was coming.

She had been betrayed.

But the safety of all the living and all the dead depended on her message getting through.

Three against one.

Her eyes narrowed and she reached into her flying jacket and took out a heavy wooden cosh. She had to escape. There was no other option.

Against all odds.

3

STAYING ALIVE

Jake Green was still alive. At first it had been easy being alive, a simple case of *not* doing deadly things. Not crossing the road without looking. Not putting your finger in the toaster. Not choosing the mystery-meat lasagne in the school canteen. Then, for a few short days a couple of months ago, it had suddenly been a lot more difficult. He had accidentally discovered he could see ghosts and subsequently been sucked into the world of the Embassy of the Dead. From that point on, staying alive needed a more proactive approach, more drastic measures like stealing a campervan and going on the run with a spectral undertaker to try and prevent Fenris the fallen reaper rising from the grave to bring forth an Age of Evil. That kind of thing.

He didn't like to think about Fenris. With the help of a few new friends, he'd pretty much condemned Fenris's spirit to an eternity trapped in a severed finger. Jake hadn't had any choice – his life had been at stake and any sort of Age of Evil had seemed best avoided, if possible. So the world had been saved and Jake Green was still alive, but weirdly, as a side effect, the Embassy of the Dead had made him an Undoer – someone who helps ghosts resolve their unfinished business on the Earthly Plane so they can continue with their onward journey to the Afterworld. It wasn't a profession he'd ever considered before and so far, despite a mysterious postcard summoning him to the Embassy of the Dead, it wasn't one he planned on following. It seemed safer to just stay at home, play video games and push the postcard to the back of his mind.

Given Jake had recently saved the world, you would think, in the grand scheme of life and death, being late for Thursday morning registration wouldn't be that important. Sadly, though, this wasn't the case. Life on the Earthly Plane went on.

And that's why he was sitting at his mum's breakfast table, shovelling cornflakes into his mouth as fast as physically possible.

His best friend Sab, sitting opposite, was tilting his phone to control a game he was playing. He was less concerned with lateness.

Jake drank the last of the cereal milk straight from the bowl. A girl's voice sounded from behind him.

'I am appalled by your complete lack of table manners.'

There was a pause. Jake placed the bowl back on the table.

'Appalled but not *at all* surprised,' the voice added flatly.

If you were blessed with the ability to see ghosts and ignored her slight transparency, Cora could have passed for an everyday schoolkid – albeit one from an exceedingly posh school, with a hockey stick in one hand and a straw boater on her head. Cora was a ghost – one of those new friends who had helped Jake take down Fenris and stay alive. Jake had freed her from the all-girls' boarding school she'd been forced to haunt since the 1990s. Now she lived in the spare bedroom of his mum's house. As a Possessor – a rare type of ghost – Cora was bound for ever to a small silver trophy from which she could venture no more than thirty or so metres. It meant she was never far away, demanding Jake take it everywhere with him, hidden in his rucksack. His only escape from her was to shut the lid. Then she was trapped inside. To be honest, he never did that. No matter how tempting it was. For one thing, he'd never hear the end of it when he opened it again. But anyway, he liked having her around, even if she was annoying. It got a bit lonely sometimes at home. He'd come to terms with the fact that his mum and dad weren't ever going to get back together. It wasn't the perfect situation, but then again it hadn't been perfect when they were together either.

Cora had promised she'd stay in her room this morning while Sab was here, but clearly she was already bored.

She leaned to one side and her hockey stick materialised from nowhere to support her weight.

'I don't know why your parents don't send you to boarding school. Then you would never be late. You might actually learn table manners too . . .'

Jake put down his bowl and wiped his mouth on his sleeve.

'You've come to talk about the postcard again, haven't you?' he asked.

Sab looked up. 'Huh?'

'Nothing. I was just talking to myself.'

Sab went back to his game. 'Idiot,' he muttered.

It was a sign of affection.

Unlike Jake, Sab was completely insensitive to the presence of ghosts. He couldn't hear or see Cora. To be honest, when he was playing a game on his phone he was pretty much insensitive to the presence of the living too. Jake was quite surprised Sab had even heard him speak.

Jake stood up and walked to the hall to get his coat.

Cora was waiting for him.

'Too right I want to talk about the postcard. It's been almost a month since we were summoned back to the Embassy of the Dead . . . It might be something important ... It might be something *fun.'*

Jake pulled a face. *Something dangerous, more like.*

He was glad to have left the Embassy of the Dead behind him. Literally everything that had happened since he'd met Stiffkey had been dangerous. And although he missed the grouchy old ghost, he was happy he'd been able to Undo the troubled undertaker and let him pass on to the Afterworld at last. Since then he'd been enjoying getting back to his life of relative normality on the Earthly Plane. Well, as normal as it could ever be when you were being nagged by a ghostly schoolgirl every day.

'Oh please can we go ...'

Jake looked up at her eager face in disbelief.

It was like she'd forgotten about Fenris. It was like she'd forgotten about Mawkins, the other reaper who, despite not being fallen and in fact being on their side in the end, had nearly sent them to the Eternal Void. And she'd definitely forgotten about the Ambassador of the Embassy of the Dead, who had been very clear in stating that, although Jake was now officially an Undoer – a member of the living blessed with the ability to help trapped spirits pass on to the Afterworld – and there was nothing she could do to prevent that, nonetheless she did not like Jake and hoped not to see him again until he was dead.

Jake couldn't even think why the Embassy had asked them back.

It *couldn't* be a good thing. And, like most of his problems, Jake felt the best way to approach it was not to approach it. Instead he had decided to ignore it. Ignore the Embassy, ignore the postcard. Ignore it *all* for as long as possible.

His mind was made up.

No, he mouthed at Cora, looking down to fasten the zip on his coat. It was time to go to school. As far as he was concerned, *the matter was closed*.

If he'd looked up, he would've seen from the look in Cora's eyes that it clearly wasn't.

Jake looked up from the exercise book on his desk where he'd been doodling the triple-crossed logo of the Embassy of the Dead in the margin. Even his subconscious seemed to be forcing it to the front of his mind. Mr French, his teacher, was standing over him with his hands on his hips. Jake quite liked Mr French – who, ironically, taught history.

Mr French frowned.

'Well, Jake. We're all waiting . . .' he said.

Jake looked around the room. His classmates' heads were all turned expectantly to him, waiting for an answer. Presumably an answer to a question he hadn't heard. He hadn't even realised the lesson had started! He looked across to Sab in panic. Sab was smiling broadly, enjoying his friend's discomfort.

'Oh dear . . .' came the familiar sound of Cora's voice.

Jake closed his eyes in disbelief and then opened them again. She was perching on Mr French's desk. He looked around the class. No one else seemed to notice her, but it was a terrible risk. She was supposed to at least *try* and be discreet when he was at school.

At least she hadn't brought Zorro with her. Zorro was a semi-wild ghost fox they'd adopted – or rather a semi-wild ghost fox that had adopted them.

He tried to ignore her and think of something to say.

That's when Zorro walked into the room.

Jake inwardly groaned.

Jake looked up at Mr French, desperately searching his face for some clue as to what he'd just said.

As if to break the awkward silence, Zorro lifted a hind leg and proceeded to wee beneath the whiteboard.

'I ... er ... w-well ...' stammered Jake, trying his best to ignore the spectral puddle that was spreading across the classroom floor.

'Come on, Jake, spit it out,' said Mr French.

The inevitable pause was broken by Cora, exasperated.

'I can't bear it!' she said from the desk. 'The

answer is *obviously* King Henry VIII's third wife, Jane Seymour.' She rolled her eyes. 'Standards of education have slipped since my day.'

Jake sighed with relief. Maybe there were advantages to having a ghost friend that no one else could see. Especially one that had almost made Head Girl and was a bit of a know-it-all.

'King Henry VIII's third wife, Jane Seymour . . .' he repeated aloud, mustering as much confidence as he could. As he reached the end of the sentence he tailed off, noticing a wicked smile creep across Cora's face.

The class dissolved into laughter, and even Mr French was struggling not to laugh.

'Really, Jake? Well I'm not sure she was at the game last night, but I'm sure if she ever did get selected to play football for England, she'd get man of the match.'

He smiled kindly at Jake.

'Anyway, that's enough about last night's football. Back to history lessons.'

Jake glared at Cora, his cheeks flushing red in a combination of embarrassment and rage.

'Can we go to the Embassy now?' she asked, still grinning.

No, he mouthed. The matter was *definitely* closed.

School had finished, and Jake was home and in the bath, trying to enjoy a normal activity that normal people did in normal, everyday life. There was a knocking from outside the bathroom. 'Are you still in there, love?' said his mum, opening the door.

'Wait!' cried Jake from the bath. He'd forgotten the lock had broken.

Still, though, what was the point of knocking and opening at the same time? That wasn't how knocking on doors was supposed to work.

'Sorry, love.' The door clicked closed.

Jake climbed out of the bath, and wrapped a towel around his middle. 'Hang on, Mum, just drying.'

'Have you put the bath mat down?'

Jake looked around for the bath mat and then down at the pool of water collecting by his feet.

'Yes,' he lied, putting the bath mat in the middle of the puddle and shifting it around with his feet to soak up the water.

'Can you let me in, love, I'm dying to use the toilet.'

'I'll be five minutes!'

Then he heard Cora's voice.

'I'm coming in too. We need to talk.'

Jake rolled his eyes, and grabbed his dressing gown, pulling it on inside out. 'So much for a normal life,' he muttered as Cora walked through the wall.

'It's about the postcard we got from the Embassy,' she began.

Jake sighed as she continued.

'I know last time was stressful for you . . .' She looked at him sympathetically. 'It's hard for someone like you . . . Jake Greens aren't supposed to be the ones saving the world. That's the kind of job a Sanderford does. We're born for it.' She looked at him modestly. 'You know my father was Lord Sanderford one of the first men to—'

'It's all right for you,' hissed Jake. 'You're already dead. I'm still alive and I kind of want to stay that way!'

15

Jake looked around as the door opened and his mum came in.

'Who are you talking to, love?' she said.

Jake groaned. 'Please, Mum!'

Was a little privacy too much to ask for?

'Oh, come on, love. You're practically fully dressed. Besides, even if you weren't, there's nothing I wouldn't have seen before when you were little.'

Cora stifled a laugh as Jake stormed from the bathroom and into his room, slamming the door behind him.

'Please, Jake,' said Cora, following him through the closed door. 'I can't go without you. You're the actual Undoer. And besides, we're a team! Righting wrongs, saving the world. Don't you miss it?'

Jake sighed.

'Look, Cora. I would go. *Honestly.* If only to get some peace and quiet from you. But it's been ages since they sent the postcard. Almost a month ... They've probably forgotten about us by now.'

Cora slumped down on the bed, waking Zorro, who had been sleeping on the pillow. He opened his eyes to check who it was and then went back to sleep. He'd spent last night chasing rabbits. A futile pursuit for a fox of no physical presence who would never be able to actually catch one. Still, he never seemed to tire of the chase.

'Do you want to watch me play a computer game?' asked Jake, trying to cheer up Cora, though he had to admit it wasn't the best offer.

Cora just sat there stroking Zorro and saying nothing.

Jake looked at her. 'They'd send for us again if they still wanted us . . . Some kind of message. And they haven't . . . So . . .'

He felt a bit guilty for some reason. It wasn't his fault Cora yearned for adventure. She was one of the only ghosts trapped on the Earthly Plane to not suffer from the 'longings' – an intense desire to reach the Afterworld. Most ghosts were trapped here due to some kind of trauma in their lifetime or death. Initially Jake had believed that Cora was a ghost because dying prevented her being made Head Girl. He soon realised she was a ghost because she had died believing she had not lived to her full potential. Only by achieving great things would she pass on to the Afterworld. And when you're as full of belief in your own potential as Cora Sanderford, that's a quite a lot of potential to fulfil!

Jake's thoughts were interrupted by his phone buzzing and he reached across to see who had texted him. Mum was in the house, so it meant it was either Sab or Dad. The only other people who ever messaged him. It was from Dad.

Hi Jake. It's Dad.

Jake rolled his eyes.

Of course it's you, Dad. You've sent the message from your own phone.

Hi

Do you know anything about this?

A picture loaded. A photo of the old shed in the field outside the farmhouse where Dad lived. It was about five minutes' drive from Mum's on the other side of the village.

> I know it's an old shed.

> On the door. The graffiti. Did you do this?

'Your dad thinks you're a graffiti artist?!' said Cora, reading over Jake's shoulder. She'd perked up a bit at the thought of Jake getting into trouble.

Jake laughed at the thought of his dad actually thinking he would ever graffiti on something. The naughtiest thing Jake had ever done was stealing biscuits from the jar in the kitchen. Well, right up until he'd had to steal his dad's campervan, but Dad didn't know about that, and besides, he'd kind of saved the world so you could argue, in that particular case, that the end justified the means.

Still, he was a bit annoyed his Dad thought he'd graffitied the shed. He tapped on his phone.

> Not me, Dad. Obviously.

Jake looked again. He couldn't see anything anyway. Just a smudge of white spray paint.

What does it say?

1 sec . . .

Another picture loaded. A close-up of the shed door. Jake swallowed, and the colour ran from his face. He tilted the phone for Cora to see the photo.

Cora's face broke into a grin. The exact opposite of the look of fear that was etched across Jake's face. On the door, roughly painted in white, was scrawled the familiar triple-crossed lines of the Embassy of the Dead.

'Some kind of message, you say?' She raised an eyebrow at Jake.

They hadn't gone to the Embassy. It seemed like the Embassy had come to them.

SOMETHING IN THE SHED

First thing the next morning, Jake and Cora walked across the fields to Dad's house. Cora was almost running with excitement; only the pull backwards towards her trophy in Jake's rucksack kept her in pace with Jake's more reluctant trudging. Zorro, as always, plodded behind them, occasionally disappearing into ditches and fields to sniff down some animal, then reappearing somewhere further up the footpath.

'Don't you feel sorry for him?' Jake asked Cora as Zorro rooted around the scattered remains of a pigeon left from the kill of a living fox. 'Always hunting but never able to catch anything.' Zorro looked up from the feathery mess with a forlorn look on his face.

'Not even something that's already dead,' Jake added, nodding towards the dead pigeon.

Cora shrugged. 'I guess it's the way of ghosts. If it were fun to be stuck on the Earthly Plane, then ghosts wouldn't get the longing to pass on to the afterlife.' She smiled. 'Death's what you make of it, I suppose.'

They climbed over the gate that led into the farmyard. Jake could see the woodshed across the farmyard, a splash of white spray paint on the door. Dad was tinkering with the engine of one of the farmer's tractors.

He wiped his hands on his overalls and walked over to Jake, beaming.

'Just in time for breakfast . . .'

He followed Jake's gaze to the old woodshed and frowned.

'Probably some teenagers,' Dad said. 'Bit weird, though. Thought you and Sab had gone bad for a minute. Started vandalising stuff.' He chuckled. 'Should've known it wasn't you. Spend all your time playing computer games. Probably do you some good to get out and about and up to some mischief.'

He put his arm round Jake's shoulder. 'Let's get those sausages on. I'm starving.'

Cora nudged Jake with the end of her hockey stick.

'You should listen to your dad. I bet he'd want you to go back to the Embassy if he knew it existed,' said Cora. 'Get up to some mischief.'

After breakfast, Jake's dad returned to his engine, and Jake and Cora walked over the field to inspect the shed door, which was locked. He'd never actually been inside, because the key to the door had been lost, long before his Dad had moved to the farm.

Jake pulled thoughtfully on the strings of his hoodie.

'What do you think it means?' he said, looking at the crudely painted symbol.

Cora flicked a stone at the door with her hockey stick, like she was scoring a goal in a very important hockey match.

'Isn't it obvious? It's a reminder, Precious ...' She walked up to the door and peered at the painted logo. Then she looked back at Jake, smiling mischievously.

'Or a warning.'

Jake joined her by the door, ignoring the nickname. She'd given it to him when they'd first met, after he'd fainted at the sight of what he'd thought was blood – actually it was ketchup, a trick she'd played on him. The ketchup had wiped off. The nickname had stuck.

Jake crouched down. Something had caught his eye. Some rainwater had puddled in a single footprint half hidden by the locked door.

It could mean only one thing. Someone had been in the shed.

He reached out and pushed the door gently with his hand. It swung inwards and he stepped back in surprise.

'It's been unlocked!' said Jake, peering cautiously into the darkness.

It was empty. Whoever had left the footprint was long gone.

A beam of winter sunlight shone through the open door, bending across the piles of rusting old farm tools, empty apple crates and broken furniture, and ending at the far end of the shed where it fell on a large pile of cloth sacks, loosely bundled in the darkness beneath a heavy wooden table. Jake's eyes settled on the table. A thermos flask was sitting on it – next to a bucket of slimy-looking water that must have been there for who knows how long.

Jake picked his way through the debris, towards the table. Pulling a large cobweb from his face, he picked up the thermos flask.

'It's warm,' he muttered to himself.

He looked around for Cora, but she had wandered off. Her voice came from around the side of the shed. 'There's probably some more instructions sprayed somewhere ... Telling us to get a move on, like we should have done a month ago!'

Jake didn't answer.

Someone had been in here. And recently. Possibly the same person that had painted the logo. But who? And what did they want with him? Could it be someone from the Embassy?

A movement on the floor caught his attention. It was the cloth sacking. One of the bags had slipped from the pile. He crouched down to pick the sack up, and a wrinkled and bony hand shot out from beneath the pile of bags, grabbing him tightly around the wrist, pulling him off balance and dragging him into the darkness.

THE VISITOR

J ake struggled against the grip. His initial yelp of fright was instantly smothered by a second hand clamping over his mouth, as a bony body pressed down against his, pinning him to the floor.

'You took your time, dear,' hissed a voice. 'Don't make a sound, the dead are lurking.'

Jake's panic subsided as he recognised the voice and, once his eyes had adjusted to the darkness, the face too, a perfect smile stretching across its wrinkled skin, revealing the artificial teeth of the woman he knew as Penny – Bad Penny, a former Undoer and, thankfully, a friend.

Well . . . a sort of friend.

She'd almost got him killed by entrusting him into the care of a soul-sucking Wight, but why let that get in the way of a rare inter-generational friendship?

She gently removed the hand from his mouth. 'Keep your trap shut, dear. There's a ghost about. I can sense a presence.'

Jake nodded. 'It's—'

Bad Penny pressed a finger to her lips.

'Sshh. Let me concentrate . . .' She closed her eyes, then sighed with relief.

'It's a child. A girl child, isn't it? One of the good ones.'

Jake shrugged. 'Most of the time.'

Bad Penny's eyes lit up. 'Is it your assistant? I was wondering who it'd be.'

'I'm not sure I'd say "assistant" to her face, to be honest. And do you think you could let me up?'

She released him from her grip and climbed out from beneath the table.

'What are you doing here, Penny?' Jake asked.

Bad Penny scowled. 'They contacted me. Needed my help to get you to go to the Embassy.'

'I thought you hated the Embassy of the Dead.'

Bad Penny shrugged. 'Well, they made me an

offer I couldn't refuse. Offered to reinstate my Undoer's Pension if I helped them out. Must be low on staff.'

Cora stepped through the barn wall and surveyed the scene.

'Who's the old lady, Precious, and why are you sitting under the table?'

'Who are you calling old?' grumbled Bad Penny.

Cora raised her eyebrows. 'She can see me!'

Bad Penny stood up and brushed the dust from her dress.

'Who's *she*? The cat's mother?'

Jake clambered out from beneath the table. 'Cora Sanderford, meet Bad Penny. As you've noticed, Penny's sensitive to the presence of ghosts. She used to be an Undoer – Stiffkey was her partner.'

Cora raised an eyebrow at this. 'And why is she in your dad's shed?'

Bad Penny smiled and pointed a bony finger at Cora.

'I like you. You remind me of a young me.' She coughed, then spat on the floor.

Then Penny turned to Jake, and the smile fell from her face. 'I like you far less.' She shook her head. 'Dragging me out all the way here. Making me stay the night in a shed. At my age too!'

Jake began to protest. 'But—'

'It doesn't do to ignore a summons from the Embassy of the Dead, Jake. It causes a lot of problems. I've had to get the train up from Worstings for one. It took ages. They're running a replacement bus service. Missed my Friday night bingo!'

She looked at her watch. 'Goodness me. It's almost time.'

'Time for what?'

'The meeting. The situation has changed since your first summons.'

'What meeting? What situation?' said Jake.

'The meeting at the Embassy,' said Bad Penny, growing impatient. 'Both your attendances are now mandatory.'

Jake looked at Cora.

'It means compulsory,' she explained.

Jake blinked.

'As in, we have to go,' she added.

30

'I know what it means! But how are we going to get there? It's a day's drive at least and I'm not stealing the campervan again.'

Bad Penny waved her hand dismissively. 'Oh, you don't have to go in person . . .' She started rummaging in her handbag. 'Only your spirit needs to go. That's why I was sent, dear. I'll help you leave your body and look after it while you're gone, then the Embassy's Summoner will pull your spirit all the way to there.'

Jake felt a chill run down his spine. His last spirit journey with Bad Penny to meet a Summoning Wight had *not* gone well.

'It's all right,' said Penny, standing up and brushing herself down. 'You'll be safe this time. The Embassy have very strict regulations and health and safety procedures in place, especially where contact between the living and Wights are concerned.'

She winked at Cora. 'Takes all the fun out of it, I reckon.'

Jake scratched his head. 'And what about my body? How will I be able to get back to it?'

'Look, dear, they asked me to do this for a reason. I know a special technique for bringing wandering souls back to their bodies.'

She took a candle from her handbag and placed it on the table between the bucket and thermos flask.

'Do we have a choice?' asked Jake.

Bad Penny frowned. 'You've got responsibilities now, Jake – you're sensitive. You've been blessed with an ability to see ghosts and there are ghosts that need helping.' She directed a bony finger at each of them in turn. 'And if they've dragged me all the way here to help you get there, it must be something important. Besides, they won't give up till they've got you, dear, so I'd save yourself some bother and go now.'

Cora smiled and thrust her hockey stick into the air triumphantly. 'Well, what are we waiting for? Two return tickets to the Embassy of the Dead, please, Penny!'

THE EMBASSY OF THE DEAD

J ake was familiar with the process of being sent on a spirit journey, but it didn't make him any less nervous as he watched Bad Penny unscrew the thermos flask and pour a cup of strange-smelling liquid into the lid.

'Some kind of potion?'

She smiled at him patiently.

'No, dear, it's Earl Grey tea.'

She took a sip and looked over at Cora.

'Just a candle for you, Jake, but she'll need something else. She doesn't have a body so she'll need something else to tether her here, else we won't be able to pull her back. Something that's personal to her. Do you have anything?'

Jake reached into his rucksack. He looked at Cora, who nodded her consent.

Jake pulled out the trophy. 'She's a Possessor,' he explained. 'Closing the lid sucks her spirit inside the trophy.'

Bad Penny turned the trophy round in her hands.

'Real silver,' she noted, raising an eyebrow.

She placed it next to the candle on the table. 'A Possessor, eh? Nice and easy for me. The Summoner will pull you from the trophy's hold. While you are in the Embassy and not strictly speaking on the Earthly Plane any more, you'll be free of its confines. I can summon you back here simply by closing the lid.'

She looked at Jake. 'And *you'll* be even simpler. I'll bring you back after an hour using my special technique.'

'What is your special technique, exactly?' asked Jake, not sure that he actually wanted the answer.

'Nothing for you to worry about, dear.' She adjusted the candle's position slightly. 'Hopefully your body will survive for an hour without your spirit.'

'Hopefully?' Jake gulped. 'Shouldn't you come with us so that you can bring us back earlier if needed?'

Bad Penny cackled. 'No. I need to stay and make sure no one steals your body. Besides, just because they're reinstating my pension doesn't mean the Embassy are welcoming me back with open arms again.'

She paused to dislodge her false teeth, wrapping them in a filthy hanky and placing them on the table.

'They put me off my humming,' she explained.

Cora looked at Jake and made a face as Bad Penny's shaky hands pulled a box of matches from her handbag and lit the candle. She stepped back and reached out for Jake's hand, her bony fingers clamping around his.

She held her hand out for Cora.

'I'm not sure I want to hold your hand,' said Cora, a little sulkily.

'She doesn't have much of a physical presence,' explained Jake. 'She can't really feel things.'

Bad Penny smiled. 'That's fine, dear. Just you place your hand near mine.'

Cora gingerly stretched out a hand, then gasped as she felt Bad Penny's fingers entwine with hers. A surprised smile crept across Cora's face.

Penny's eyes sparkled. 'You're not an Undoer for fifty years without learning some tricks,' she said proudly. 'I was the best of my generation!'

Cora smiled at her. 'You remind me of an older version of me,' she said.

Bad Penny started to hum, and Jake and Cora stared into the candlelight, the dancing shadows it cast merging together, until the interior of the shed slipped away into the darkness that surrounded the flame. The light grew brighter and bigger until it burnt Jake's eyes and he was forced to close them.

'Whoa! That was quick for a living spirit!!' said a man's voice.

Jake slowly opened his eyes. Blinking in the light of a single suspended electric bulb, Jake saw that Bad Penny and Cora and the shed had disappeared. He must have arrived at the Embassy of the Dead – or at least his spirit had. He shuddered at the thought of his actual body, sitting lifeless, many miles away, in a cobwebby shed.

Jake took in his new surroundings. He was sitting in an uncomfortable plastic chair, at a small table, in a small windowless room. The table was pushed up against a glass partition that split the room in two. On the other side of the glass sat the man who had spoken. He was tall with a straggling, wild beard sprouting from high up his sunken, sunburnt face. Tattoos climbed up and around his long skinny arms until they disappeared beneath the rolled-up sleeves of a Hawaiian shirt. A tattered, too-small sun hat was perched on top of his head. He looked like he'd just returned from a beach holiday that had lasted about twenty years.

'Good to see you, man,' he said, holding up a form to the glass. 'Apparently you have to sign this.' He pointed to a space on the form then pushed it through a thin slot in the glass. 'They like forms here, don't they!'

Jake picked up a pen from the table. It was one of those ones that was tied to the table with a coil of plasticky wire. He signed his name, and slid the form back through the slot before realising he probably should have read the document first.

The man put his hand to his mouth and made a short choking noise. Like he had a hair caught in his throat.

'Are you OK?' asked Jake.

The man nodded and wiped his beard on his Hawaiian shirt.

'It's nothing.' He smiled, and pushed a small ticket through the gap in the glass.

Jake picked it up and looked at it. It was a cloakroom ticket, with the number 591 on it.

The last time Jake had been given one of these tickets was when he'd arrived at the Embassy of the Dead by campervan and been forced to 'leave his life at the door' by Eustace the cloakroom attendant. Eustace was a Bodyshifter who could remove souls from the living and occupy their bodies – a good skill to have when needing to carefully 'walk' bodies to the cloakroom for storage. Eustace had given him a ticket that Jake had assumed could be exchanged for the return of his body. But it turned out it had another purpose too. It was a ticket that counted down the time he had left in the Embassy of the Dead before his spirit would be unable to rejoin his body.

It felt strange to be there again. A weird nauseous feeling to be exact. Jake wasn't sure if it was a side effect of having left his body, or a result of the anxiety he felt about being back in the Embassy of the Dead. Maybe a mix of both – with a dash of excitement thrown in because, despite himself, despite his earlier reluctance to return to the Embassy, he felt a weird sense of belonging. Maybe Bad Penny was right? Maybe this was his calling?

'Where's Cora?' he asked the Wight.

'The ghost that just got here? She's already been processed. Much quicker for me to get a spirit that's already been separated from its body for a while. Living spirits are more –' his eyes rolled in their sockets like he was searching for the right word – 'more . . . *sticky*,' he finished.

Jake nodded politely as the man continued.

'You were fast though. Are you sure you're not dead?'

'I hope not,' muttered Jake.

The Wight reached forward to a tin of mints on his desk and popped one in his mouth.

39

'They help take my mind off how delicious your spirit energy would taste,' he explained.

He laughed, and Jake joined in nervously.

'Are you the Summoner'

The man leant back on his chair and put his flip-flop-clad feet on the desk.

'Yup. Guilty as charged! That's why I'm behind the glass. So I can't get to you! Otherwise I'd suck out your energy. Can't help myself!' He pulled a mock scary face. 'Don't let Herman touch you, else he'll take your soul.'

Jake smiled nervously again. 'Why have I been summoned?'

'Well, *I* heard –' he looked around the office secretively – '*someone's* gone missing!'

There was the sound of raised voices from behind the door.

'What do you mean he's in there alone?' a voice boomed. Then the muttering of an explanation, followed by more shouting. *'I don't care about the glass. No one should be left alone with Herman Poltago . . . Especially not a LIVING CHILD.'*

40

Herman rolled his eyes, then leaned right forward and whispered, 'But you didn't hear it from me.' And winked. Jake smiled. He couldn't help but like the Wight – despite the soul-sucking part.

The door opened and Jake looked up to see a man dressed in military uniform and a cap. A row of medals was pinned on his chest. Jake immediately recognised the ghost known as the Captain. This was the Embassy of the Dead's second in command – the Ambassador's right-hand man. Jake had met him the only other time he'd visited the Embassy, when the Captain and the Ambassador and her personal assistant, Maureen, had arrived to clean up the messy business of Fenris's missing finger and scold Jake for not getting it to them sooner. Why was he here now? Surely the Captain was far too important to be bothering with Jake?

'Hello, Cap'n,' said Herman from behind the glass screen, saluting comically. He started to giggle and then choked slightly. He put his hand to his mouth and pulled out what looked suspiciously like some seaweed. He dropped it in a wastepaper bin then wiped his hand on his shirt.

The Captain glowered at Herman through the glass, then turned to Jake. 'What on earth took you so long? You were summoned weeks ago. Come with me, Green. No time to lose. Quick march.' Then spinning on his heels, he limped from the room. 'Once a Wight, always a Wight,' he muttered loud enough for Jake and Herman Poltago to hear.

Jake nodded an apologetic goodbye to Herman and followed the Captain from the room and into another larger room dominated by a large polished wooden table. All around the room paintings in lavish gilt frames were hung.

The Captain waved at the walls as he passed. 'Portraits of former Ambassadors . . .'

Jake looked at a picture of a bearded man in mayoral robes, labelled with a name, a birthdate, a death date and a passing to the Afterworld date.

The Captain paused, and smiled.

'Sir Hildebrand Gautner. The first Ambassador,' he explained. He turned in a slow circle, respectfully taking in the portraits of the all the previous Ambassadors, before settling on a portrait of a woman.

'And of course, you'll recognise the current Ambassador.'

Jake nodded. Her scowling face haunted his memory. Even in her portrait, she looked like she was just about to tell him off.

The Captain walked through another door on the other side of the room and out into a long, wood-panelled corridor. Jake was glad to escape the current Ambassador's disapproving gaze. Despite the Captain's limp, Jake had to break into a trot to keep up with his purposeful stride.

'Did Herman tell you how he died?' asked the Captain, glancing back over his shoulder.

'I didn't like to ask,' replied Jake.

'Damn fool fell off a yacht,' said the Captain. 'Slipped on a literal banana skin – would you believe? Banged his head and passed out before plunging into the brine.'

Jake blinked. It was hard to know what to say.

'Of course the seaweed's a problem,' continued the Captain. 'He brings up a kilo a day, I'd wager. Small fish sometimes too.' He chuckled. 'Poor blighter.' The Captain looked at Jake from beneath bushy eyebrows. The smile dropped from his face. He looked at Jake. 'Did he tell you anything about why you're here?'

Jake heard Herman's words again in his mind. *Someone's gone missing . . .*

But there was something about the Captain's expression that told Jake that Herman would get into trouble if he mentioned this.

Jake shook his head.

The Captain's smile returned. 'In my day we would never have employed a Wight. You can't trust them. But the current Ambassador's all about involving all types of ghostkind.'

He turned a corner and Jake scampered to catch up. 'People's lives and deaths are very interesting,' said the Captain. 'One should never be shy to ask a ghost how they died.'

There was an awkward pause, before Jake took the Captain's hint.

'How did you die?' asked Jake.

'Shot.' He pointed to a gap in the row of medals across his chest. 'Awarded a posthumous Victoria Cross though. The poor blighters were expecting us to attack at dawn and we took them down at midnight. A dirty trick, but worked a treat! We won the battle and eventually the war, although I didn't live to see it.' He smiled at Jake. 'Always turn up early for a fight. Especially if it means your enemy are asleep!'

He opened the door and Jake followed him into a grand assembly hall full of people sitting facing an empty stage.

'Find a seat, lad. Jump to it. The Ceremony's about to begin.'

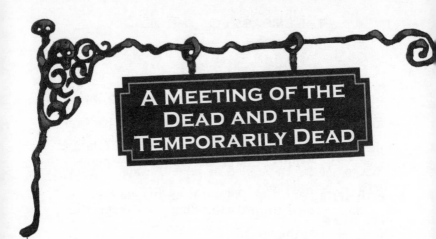

A MEETING OF THE DEAD AND THE TEMPORARILY DEAD

For a moment Jake was lost. Then he saw someone waving. It was Cora. She'd saved him a seat near the back of the room.

As he made his way over to her, he took in the people gathered in the packed-out hall. Jake estimated there were probably around sixty people. It was hard to tell who was dead and who, like him, was just temporarily dead. In the Embassy, all ghosts, and spirits of the living, had full visibility and a solid form. He took his seat next to Cora. He looked across at her and noticed she had a light sprinkling of freckles across the bridge of her nose, something that didn't usually show up on her usually half-transparent face.

She looked at Jake looking at her. 'What?'

'Nothing,' he said, nodding a polite hello to a short, stocky postman who was sitting on the other side of him. 'Do you know what's going on?' he whispered to Cora.

Cora shook her head. 'I've got no idea, but whatever it is must be important for all these people to be here. And look . . .'

She nodded towards the door as a respectful hush fell over the crowd.

A line of persons, both living and dead, were entering the hall and filing on to the stage, taking their seats on a row of chairs at the front.

The postman glanced at Jake and smiled nervously.

'They're the Elite Undoers and their ghost assistants . . .' he whispered excitedly.

Jake looked at the line of ghosts. First up was a short, bespectacled elderly man sitting next to a woman with a colourful headscarf wound high on her head.

'That's Edward Stapleton, or "Death" as they call him on account of how long he's been at this, and that's his ghost assistant, Alice Tambajang.'

Jake's eyes scanned along the row of serious-looking people. Next up was a stick-thin lady sitting next to the ghost of what must have been her identical twin. Then came a barrel-chested man with a large square beard sitting next to the ghost of what appeared to be a chimney sweep. He was next to a stern-looking woman and a finely dressed gentleman in a bowler hat.

'She must've been a ghost for ages,' whispered Jake, noticing the lady's old-fashioned clothes.

The postman chuckled. 'No, she was actually quite a famous actor. Only recently dead. You can tell by her trainers.'

'Idiot,' said Cora, nudging Jake. She was enjoying having a physical presence.

Finally Jake's eyes settled on the figure next to

the finely dressed gentleman. She was tall with long black hair, about the same age as his mum perhaps, and wearing a formal-looking black dress.

'Who's that?' asked Cora, leaning across Jake to ask the postman, who seemed to know everyone.

Without asking who she meant, the postman whispered, 'That's Portentia. Isn't she beautiful!'

Cora pulled an unimpressed face.

'Where's her assistant?' asked Jake, noticing the empty chair to the other side of her.

The postman frowned. 'I don't know. She should be here . . . Amber Chase. The former test pilot. She crashed outside Tangiers in 1928 on an experimental long-range flight . . .'

'Cool!' whispered Cora. 'Being a test pilot, I mean. Not the crashing bit obviously,' she added.

Jake blinked. 'How do you know all this stuff?'

The postman blushed, proudly.

'I'm just a big geek when it comes to Undoers. Still can't believe I'm actually going to be one!'

The last seat was slightly separate from the others. On it sat a large man who was holding his head beneath his arm.

Before Jake had a chance to enquire about him, a woman in jodhpurs, boots and a riding hat clopped on to the wooden stage. The room immediately fell silent.

It was the Ambassador of the Embassy of the Dead – the most powerful ghost on the Earthly Plane – and she looked even more disapproving than her portrait.

The Ambassador stood, hands on hips, staring out at the audience as if challenging them to say something. Certainly no one in the audience looked as if they wanted to take up that challenge.

Jake turned to face the front, and the Ambassador began to speak.

'Friends. You may be wondering why you've been summoned here . . .' There was a shuffling and nodding of heads among the crowd. 'A large part of the role of the Embassy of the Dead has always been, and will always be, to protect the interests of spirits trapped on the Earthly Plane. And I'm pleased to welcome some of you here today.' She motioned to the crowd. There was a ripple of applause.

The postman turned to Jake. 'That's the Ambassador,' he whispered excitedly, distracting Jake from the Ambassador's speech. 'She's in charge of the whole Embassy . . .'

Jake nodded impatiently. He was trying to listen.

'. . . And also welcome to those of you who are still living. The Undoers.' She smiled humourlessly. 'May your souls pass peacefully to the Afterworld when the time comes for you to shuffle off this mortal coil.'

'Mortal what?' whispered Jake to Cora.

'It's a quote from Shakespeare, dummy. Don't your teachers teach you anything?'

Jake shrugged.

The postman nudged Jake again and pointed proudly to himself. '*I'm* an Undoer!' He reached over to shake Jake's hand. 'Geoff, by the way. Pleased to meet you . . .?'

'Jake,' whispered Jake, shaking the man's clammy hand whilst not looking away from the stage.

The Ambassador was still talking. 'Some of you gathered here are what we refer to as our reserve force. Namely, those members of the living who have obtained the status of Undoer, but have not yet, for various reasons, been called into official action. Well, today is that hallowed day. We live in dangerous times. The threat of Fenris may have been neutralised –' the Ambassador's eyes skirted over Jake's dismissively – 'for now. But rebel forces faithful to Fenris and his mission to break down the walls that keep the living and the dead apart are gaining in strength and numbers, and they are always on the lookout for new ways to penetrate the Earthly Plane and bring it under their order. We must remain vigilant. Due to a recent –' she paused to think of the correct word – 'situation, the details of which are not important . . .'

Jake and Cora's eyes met for a split second. No way was it *'not important'*.

Jake leant over and whispered. 'I heard that *someone* is missing.'

Cora raised an eyebrow. 'They're probably going to ask us to help find them . . . You know, because we saved the whole world last time.'

The Ambassador continued. '. . . We have been forced to reassign our Elite Undoers –' she gestured to the people standing on the stage – 'to new duties. We have therefore summoned you here to temporarily take over the job of Undoing.'

Geoff the postman nudged Jake. 'We're going to be assigned ghosts to Undo! That means working out why they became a ghost and undoing that problem.'

Jake rolled his eyes. 'I *know*,' he hissed, then immediately felt bad.

Geoff looked a little hurt. He smiled sadly. 'Sorry. I get a bit excited, sometimes. My wife says, *Geoff, stop working yourself up into a lather.*' He smiled sadly. 'She's not sensitive to the presence of ghosts, though. Doesn't even believe in them.'

For the first time Jake took a look at the man sitting next to him. He was short for a grown-up. About Jake's height, with curly reddish hair receding away from a doughy face. He smiled at Jake. 'It's our chance now. It's our chance to be Undoers! I've been waiting to be summoned for years – I can't believe it's really happening!' He clapped his hands together excitedly.

Meanwhile the Ambassador was still talking.

'Some of you are yet to have been sworn in ... We'll precede with that at once. You'll be given your official licence and Undoer codename and then assigned to an outstanding case.'

Cora folded her arms. 'So we're just the reserves!' she huffed. 'Helping some stuffy old ghost move on to the Afterworld. Just filling in while someone else gets to do the exciting, secret stuff.'

Jake sighed with relief. At least there would be no reapers involved this time.

The Ambassador continued. 'Remember, whatever ... situations the Embassy faces, our primary mission must continue. Spirits trapped on the Earthly Plane need to pass to the Afterworld. The system must not be compromised!' She looked across the crowd, and for a moment, to Jake at least, her eyes seemed to settle on him alone.

'Don't let me down.'

THE CEREMONY

The first person to be called to the stage was a professor of mathematics. A scruffy, middle-aged woman with a keen face, she stepped up to the stage in her battered corduroy suit, and listened attentively while the Ambassador listed her living achievements – most of which Jake didn't really understand.

'Now,' said the Ambassador, 'please repeat after me the Undoer's oath.'

The professor nodded, and the Ambassador began to speak.

'I swear to protect the living from the dead and the dead from the living and uphold the laws that keep their worlds apart.'

The professor repeated the oath solemnly, before being presented with a card, which Jake assumed must be her licence, a book, and a small, ornate box.

Then the Ambassador explained that the professor would be given her codename by a representative of the Afterworld Authorities. 'If you would be so kind, Minister Tokelo Fortune,' she said.

The man with his head under his arm stood up, walked to the front of the stage and placed his head on the table. The head looked around the audience.

Jake wondered how a man in an ill-fitting suit had come to have his head cleanly severed from his shoulders, and by the look on the audience's faces, Jake reckoned that this question was on everybody's mind.

The body stood still behind the head. And the audience fell into complete silence as the head began to speak.

'It falls upon me, Minister Tokelo Fortune, to bestow upon you a name – a name reserved only for the use of the Embassy. A name that tethers you to your duty for the rest of your life . . .'

He looked over the room, revelling in the effect his words were having.

The audience held its breath.

'Professor . . .' Minister Tokelo Fortune closed his eyes. Jake could see his eyeballs swivelling wildly behind closed eyelids. 'I see great battles ahead. Battles of the mind. Your name will be . . . "Rook". A bird associated with death, and a key piece on a chess board, one of your favourite games, I believe.'

'Rook! That's a cool name,' whispered Cora. 'I wonder what your name will be . . .'

Jake felt himself getting excited in spite of himself. The ceremony was starting to get interesting. 'It's a bit like that scene in *Harry Potter* with the sorting hat . . .'

Cora looked puzzled. 'Harry Potter? Who's he?'

Jake blinked. 'You need to get out more.'

She glared at him. Sometimes Jake forgot she'd been trapped in a silver trophy since the early 1990s.

The professor smiled at the sound of her Undoer's name, obviously pleased with the moniker

'Rook'. She bowed politely at the Ambassador and Tokelo Fortune, and was ushered back to her seat next to her ghostly assistant, a youngish man in a baseball cap.

It could be assumed that those living people blessed with the ability to see and speak to ghosts might have something else special about them. And to Jake, at the beginning of the ceremony, it definitely seemed that way.

After the professor had come business leaders, architects, surgeons, high-ranking politicians, even a former Olympic gymnast – people of some note on the Earthly Plane. All swearing the oath, being given a codename, a card, the book, and a small wooden box.

Then, as the ceremony continued, the jobs became more normal – teachers, nurses, a school caretaker.

Jake squirmed in his seat. It was like picking teams at football all over again. Not blessed with natural sporting talent, he was familiar with the creeping sense of embarrassment he felt as the room emptied.

Soon almost everyone in the room had been to the stage. Everyone apart from Jake and Geoff.

'This is so cringy. They're leaving the worst till last. They must think you two are useless ...' muttered Cora. 'No offence,' she added, smiling sweetly across at the postman.

'None taken,' he said, smiling back. 'I'm just happy to be here.'

The postman's ghost assistant was sitting behind him, a tiny old lady dozing over her knitting needles, who woke up at the sound of his name being called from the stage. 'Geoff Inkhurst!'

Moments later, he'd sworn the oath and been given his name – Stamp.

Jake's was the very last name to be called. He walked to the stage and up the stairs towards the Ambassador.

She smiled coldly at him. 'We meet again ...' she said, without emotion. 'Repeat after me ...'

Jake uttered the oath, taking care not to stumble over any of the words. He didn't want to give the ‵mbassador any more reason to think he was an ‵. Then she handed him a book, a small, blank, black card, and a wooden box, about the size of a large matchbox. He held them nervously in his sweaty hands.

Again, Minister Fortune closed his eyes. It seemed to Jake to last for ever. He mentally crossed his fingers.

Tokelo Fortune's eyes began to roll, and for a moment he grimaced as though in pain. He let out a loud and dramatic groan that filled the room.

Jake shifted uncomfortably on the stage as Minister Fortune finally opened his eyes after blinking a few times, a look of genuine surprise on his face.

'Well, well, well . . .' he said. 'I name you . . .'

He paused, eyeing Jake strangely.

'I name you Wormling.'

Jake felt himself go bright red, and heard the poorly supressed laughter of the audience.

Wormling?

It *definitely* wasn't the name he was hoping

WORMLING

After the ceremony, Jake and Cora were ushered from the room, joining the other reserve Undoers in a long corridor. It became apparent that they were to wait there until they were called for some kind of individual briefing. Once again it seemed as ~~~ugh they were being called from most to least ~~~

~~~d.

~~~nling was at the bottom of the list.

~~~eren't enough chairs for all the new ~~~ the corridor so Jake and Cora had ~~~ right at the end, and were sitting ~~~d like they'd been waiting for ~~~ew Undoers wasn't getting ~~~ket from his pocket. The

'Bad Penny said we only had an hour,' said Jake anxiously. 'I don't suppose the Embassy would let me stay here so long I'd die?'

Cora just shrugged, seemingly unfazed by the idea Jake might die. She reached out for the book that lay on the floor next to him. 'Can I have a look?' she asked, and Jake, unable to think of a good reason why not, reluctantly passed the book over.

She picked it up and started to read out a chapter heading. '*Government and Economics within the Afterworld.* 'Crikey, that sounds a little dry.'

She flicked to the contents page. 'These sound more like it . . .' Her finger traced down the chapters, reading aloud. '7.2 Gargoyles, 7.3 Demons, 7.4 Bonewulf . . .'

Jake sighed. He'd had enough bonewulf to last him a lifetime.

'Jake Green?' Maureen, the Ambassador's assistant, was approaching, clipboard in hand.

Jake jumped up. 'Yes?'

She turned to Cora, who leapt up too. 'Cora Sanderford? This way, please.'

She led them through a door, and down another

long corridor. The Embassy of the Dead was like a rabbit warren. Jake had been there before of course, but the layout was confusing. It was far larger than it appeared on the outside, and the corridors didn't seem to follow any sort of logic.

'Wait in there,' said Maureen, pointing to a door with a new-looking brass plaque with 'Wilkinson' on it. 'He'll be about ten minutes.' She walked off, not looking up from her clipboard.

Jake pushed open the door and entered a tiny office with an immaculately ordered desk.

'It's very clean in here,' said Jake, eyeing a row of pencils ordered by size and lined up perfectly perpendicular to the edge of the desk.

'Unlike your bedroom,' said Cora.

Jake was just about to protest when he noticed Cora wandering casually back out the door.

He jumped up and went after her. '*Cora!*' he hissed. She was standing in the doorway of the room opposite, which appeared to be a small library.

'Look at all these books,' she muttered, taking a dusty-looking volume from the shelves. '*Talking Crow: A Guide to Corvine Conversation.*'

'Cora, we're not supposed to be in here! We should be waiting in the office!' said Jake.

Cora looked at him with a mischievous gleam in her eyes and he realised he'd made a terrible mistake.

Never tell Cora she's not allowed to do something.

'I suppose we're not allowed in here either?' she said, skipping over to the far side of the room and opening another door and stepping through.

'*Cora!*' hissed Jake again. He scampered through the library after her and into the next room. 'Come back!'

'Stop worrying!' said Cora. 'We've got ten minutes. The Clipboard Dragon said so!'

Jake looked around the room. Leaning against the far wall he noticed two large pinboards covered with photographs and Post-it notes. In front of them, facing the display, were twenty or so chairs. Cora was examining one of the boards.

'Didn't you say someone was missing?' she asked. 'I think I know who it is.' Jake reluctantly came over to see what she was talking about. Cora pointed to a series of photos pinned on the board. 'I

think it's the ghost assistant of that Undoer ...
What was her name?'

'Portentia,' said Jake, remembering the beautiful
lady with the empty chair next to her. He looked at
the wall of pictures. One was of a black and white
photo of a pilot – a girl pilot – standing in front of a
biplane. The next was a close-up of the same girl,
her curly hair forcing its way from beneath a leather
flying cap. She was giving the photographer a bored
expression, like she had better things to do than
pose for a photo.

'Remember what the postman said? He said
Portentia's ghost assistant was a pilot.'

Jake nodded distractedly. Above the photos
was a Post-it note, on which was written in large
letters: *WHERE IS SHE?*

Then Jake's eyes settled on a row of photos
beneath those of the pilot. Some of the photos were
of unusual-looking but clearly very valuable
jewellery, but others were of less obvious value – a
collection of black stones, a crystal mounted on a
marble base, a tiny jug covered in strange markings
that looked like it had been carved from bone. All of

them had been laid on a white table and photographed next to a ruler to show their size.

Just then there was the sound of voices and approaching footsteps.

Jake looked at Cora in panic.

'*What do we do?*' he hissed. His eyes darted around the room. There was no other exit.

'Quick, behind the pinboards,' he gasped, grabbing Cora by the hand and pulling her into the small space between them and the wall. The pinboard wobbled slightly and Cora steadied it with her hand just as someone entered the room. Between the two boards was a tiny crack, just big enough to peek through. Jake pressed his eye to the crack and groaned inwardly.

It was the Ambassador.

I'LL BE BRIEF

Jake's heart was beating so hard, it was clattering against his ribcage. He scowled at Cora. *This was all her fault, as usual!* But there was nothing they could do now except be as silent as they could and sit it out.

There was the sound of other people entering the room and taking seats. Then the Ambassador's voice sounded loudly over the din and with every word she spoke Jake felt himself sink deeper and deeper into danger.

'As you all know, Amber Chase is missing. A quick recap if you please, Maureen, for those Undoers we've just pulled on to this case.'

Through the crack, Jake could see the backs of the Ambassador's and Maureen's heads addressing the group of seated Undoers. Jake could just about make out that they were the ones that had been on the stage – the Elite Undoers.

Maureen started to speak.

'I'll be brief. Amber Chase: experimental test pilot in life, skilled in hand-to-hand combat, expert marksman ... markswoman, I mean. Missing now for almost a month under what can only be described as deeply suspicious circumstances ... Portentia?'

There was the sound of a chair scraping and a softer, quietly confident voice began to talk.

Jake shifted his position so he could see the speaker. It was the lady from the stage in the black dress. *Portentia.*

'Chase has been my spectral assistant for five years, and I know her better than anyone, but a month ago ... Something changed. And shortly after, she disappeared. We know that she had become ... intrigued by a gang involved in the continuing illegal trade in artefacts from the Afterworld on the Earthly Plane.'

There was the sound of muttering.

Portentia turned to address the gathered Undoers. 'Chase was supposedly following a lead in

London when she disappeared. After an absence of two days we alerted the Embassy. A search was carried out in her Embassy quarters. We found these Afterworld artefacts, all reported stolen in the Afterworld.' She tapped on the pinboard. 'It seems she got a little bit too involved with the smugglers.'

She was so close that Jake could smell her perfume. He shrank back from the crack he was peering through.

A croaky voice spoke from the crowd. Jake assumed it was Stapleton, the old man from the stage. The man they knew as Death.

'It's a disgrace. How a member of the Embassy could—'

Portentia continued over the top of the old man. 'In short, we believe Chase is working with the smugglers—'

The Ambassador's voice interrupted. 'And any leads on who these smugglers are?'

'Nothing solid,' Portentia replied. 'Most likely strays. We are following up on a number of leads.'

Jake looked at Cora. *Strays?* What did that mean? Cora shrugged.

The Ambassador started to speak again. 'Well. It's not much to go on, frankly. But it's all we have for now. I'll have Maureen distribute a file to each of you. This is our current priority. Find Amber Chase and bring her in. Portentia will be taking the lead here, and the Captain will be handling the new Undoers who'll be covering your usual Undoing duties until Amber Chase is found and brought to justice. For now, it's only missing artefacts we're investigating, but who knows where this could lead, what the enemy might try to smuggle on to the Earthly Plane next. The forces of Fenris cannot be trusted and will exploit any weaknesses in our resolve. Traitors must be flushed out as soon as possible.'

Stapleton stood, his croaking voice breaking the silence once more. 'The Embassy has stood strong for many years and will stand strong for many more.'

The Ambassador frowned. 'That's as may be, but let me remind you, the minority of celestial beings that follow the way of Fenris are growing in power and they won't stop until they overturn the rule of the Afterworld Authorities. They seek nothing less than to take the spirits of the living and the dead as their slaves. At the moment their activity has been limited to acts of sabotage, but their attacks are increasing in intensity. The Authorities are beginning to suffer. Their grip on the Afterworld is weakening. The Embassy's influence on the Earthly Plane is weakening too. Shadowfolk have been sighted here, moving unseen amongst the living. Last time we were lucky . . . Let's not leave anything to chance this time. That will be all.'

There was the sound of scraping chairs and people leaving the room.

Jake and Cora remained as still as they could, waiting for silence. Jake pressed his eye to the gap once more. To his horror he saw that the Ambassador was approaching the pinboard, and seemed to be looking directly at him. He froze in terror, sure she had seen him.

'If there's one thing I can't stand it's people betraying the Embassy,' she said. Jake's heart was pumping so hard in his chest that it seemed like the noise would deafen him. But then the Ambassador spun on her heels, and marched from the room. Jake sighed, letting out the huge breath he'd been holding. He felt dizzy with relief. He turned to glare at Cora.

'You are going to get us both killed one day.'

Cora smiled sweetly. 'Correction: I'm going to get *you* killed. I'm already dead, remember!'

WORK PHONE

s soon as they were sure the coast was clear, Jake and Cora rushed back to the room they were supposed to be waiting in. To their relief, they found it still empty. They slumped down into the chairs, glad to wait in peace, unable to believe that they'd escaped detection . . .

The door opened behind them.

'Have you looked in the spectral container yet?' said a neatly dressed man bustling in carrying a large pile of papers. He scampered round his desk and placed them in a pile. Then he sat down and pointed to a name tag on his desk.

'The name's Wilkinson,' he said with a broad smile. 'How long have you got?'

Jake looked at his ticket with a start. He had

completely forgotten to check. The number had dropped to 20.

'Twenty . . . erm, twenty somethings.'

The man named Wilkinson nodded. 'That should be fine.' He leant over the desk, his eyes shining in excitement. 'So . . . have you looked in the spectral container yet?' It took Jake a moment to realise that he meant the box.

Jake was less excited. Last time he had opened a box from the Embassy he had found himself responsible for a finger containing the trapped spirit of a fallen reaper who was intent on bringing about the Age of Evil. Jake was understandably reluctant this time. He shook his head.

Wilkinson rubbed his hands together and leaned forward to look at the small box in Jake's hand.

'It's a lovely bit of kit. *Vintage.* Second best thing you get issued as an Undoer. The Embassy have switched back to the old system for the reserve Undoers. More secure than a mobile phone or a spectral communicator,' he said. 'Cheaper to run, too.'

Jake cautiously pulled open the drawer of the box. He recoiled as he saw the contents: held in place by a single strip of elastic was the slightly dehydrated corpse of a mouse! It looked as though it had been run over by a careless cyclist fifty years ago. And it smelt . . . musty. Next to the dead mouse was a button.

Jake closed the drawer sharply and screwed his eyes shut in frustration.

'Can't it ever just be something *normal*?' He passed the box to Cora, who was pawing at him in her keenness to see what was in it.

She opened it and took a look. 'Cool!'

The man leant forward towards Cora. 'Now, watch this!' he said, barely able to conceal his excitement. He pointed to a switch on his desk and, after a long pause for effect, he flicked it to the 'on' position.

The dead mouse opened its eyes and blinked.

Jake looked across the desk in horror at Wilkinson. '*It's alive?*'

Wilkinson smiled and gave Jake a thumbs up. Inside the box the mouse grimaced and raised its tiny front legs, in a crude approximation of Wilkinson's gesture.

Wilkinson turned his thumbs up into a wave.

The mouse waved.

'It . . . it copies what you're doing?' stammered Jake.

Wilkinson nodded, beaming from ear to ear. 'Yes. Whoever sits on the chair can control the actions of the mouse. The switch on the desk is charged with old magic. It transfers a tiny fraction of the spirit of whomsoever flicks the switch into the body of the dead mouse. Essentially, I'm inhabiting its corpse. It's really *very* clever.'

He twisted what looked like a volume control next to the switch.

'That's not all!' he said, smiling broadly.

'That's not all!' said the mouse in a small, strangled voice.

Cora burst into laughter. Jake gave her a withering look. 'Does the mouse know it's doing this?'

Wilkinson leant over and flicked the switch to off and the mouse flopped back into its contorted position.

'Not at all. Its spirit has long passed to the Afterworld ... It is merely an empty vessel.' He straightened the already straight row of pencils on his desk. 'So! As you may have guessed, I'm your handler at the Embassy. And this is how we will communicate. You'll receive instruction through your Necrommunicator.' He indicated towards the mouse.

Jake sighed. 'Does it have a ringtone?' he asked. 'I mean, when you want to contact me?'

Wilkinson smiled. 'Not really. I'll just turn it on and call your name.'

He leant forward and pointed to the button next to the mouse. 'And you can press this if you need to contact me. Emergencies only though.'

Wilkinson started searching through the papers on his desk and gathered a handful. 'Your first case,' he said, handing the wodge of paper to Jake.

Jake had seen the like before. At Bad Penny's house. He could remember seeing Cora's file for the first time. The Embassy official who had audited her had got her completely wrong. They had thought she had no visible presence, not even to Undoers.

Just a poltergeist making her old trophy clatter around to scare pupils. In fact, though, she *was* visible. She was a *Possessor*, trapped inside her trophy, until Jake had let her out. Jake looked at the file he'd just been given, and hoped this ghost didn't have the same auditor.

He began to read aloud. '*Errol Clay b.1930 – d.1980. Type: Spectre. Visible presence: Minor (0.3).* At least I'll be able to see him . . . just,' he muttered. '*Physical form: Medium (0.5).*'

Jake frowned. That might be enough to physically harm him. Cora's presence was so slight that she could pass through walls as if they weren't there. Apart from her hockey stick, she could barely interact with the Earthly Plane at all.

'*Reports of a figure seen roaming the former site of Clay's Snooker Club in Redchapel Street, London . . .*'

Wilkinson shuddered. 'London!' he muttered. 'Dreadful place. Full of strays!'

'What are strays?' Jake asked. It was that word again. The word that Portentia had used in the briefing.

'Ghosts who haven't been audited by the Embassy. They tend to gather in cities, I'm afraid. Bad crowd. Ghosts tend to go wrong without the levelling influence of the Embassy.'

'I thought all ghosts were audited by the Embassy?'

Wilkinson shook his head. 'No system is perfect. There's always some who fall through the net.'

Jake nodded and continued to read. '*Reports of a figure seen roaming the former site of Clay's Snooker Club in Redchapel Street, London, have been confirmed as the spectre of Errol Clay, a former career criminal who died during a botched armed robbery on Christmas Eve 1980. Errol Clay believes he was betrayed by his own brother, Ethan, and haunts the site of the former snooker club they co-owned. We believe that the emotional trauma of the betrayal has caused his haunting. Solution: Unknown.*'

Wilkinson took a hanky from his pocket and blew his nose loudly.

Jake ignored him and continued reading. '*So far, contrary to his life, Errol Clay has caused no harm to the living.*' Jake blinked. *So far!* '*Priority: Low.*'

Then there was a scrawled signature of the ghost that had originally assessed the spectre of Errol Clay.

Ezekiel Frost, Ghost Auditor, the Embassy of the Dead.

The same ghost that had audited Cora incorrectly.

Jake sighed, then carried on reading. '*Assigned Undoer – ~~Portentia~~ Wormling.*'

Wilkinson smiled. 'It's one of Portentia's Undoings. A tricky one probably as she's had this case active for a while.' He looked serious for a second. 'She's otherwise engaged at the moment, as you know. Hence why we've employed you two.'

'I didn't see her partner today,' said Cora innocently. 'Is she around?'

Wilkinson stood up. 'That's classified,' he said firmly. 'That will be all for now.'

Cora raised a slight eyebrow at Jake as they stood to leave. As Jake gathered up his papers, he thought of something. 'What about the other bit of kit?' asked Jake. 'You said the Necro-whatever-it-is was the *second* best.'

Wilkinson smiled. 'Goodness me. I almost forgot!' He turned and took something metal from the shelf.

'A genuine 1987 *Rexel Matador*. Look at that lovely dull sheen. It takes three hundred 25mm rounds and fits snugly in your pocket. A highly efficient little number. An essential weapon in your Undoer armoury.'

'And I'm allowed to use it?' asked Jake anxiously.

Wilkinson looked confused. 'Of course you are. It's a stapler. It staples your papers together.' He took the bundle of papers from Jake and neatly stapled them, before handing them and the stapler back. 'You don't want to get them in the wrong order!'

Wilkinson motioned to the door. 'We'll leave the rest up to you.' He picked up Jake's box from the table and handed it to him. 'Remember to keep this with you at all times. In case of danger. We wouldn't want you getting lost.'

'Lost?'

Wilkinson nodded. 'Yes. It's a euphemism. We handlers use it instead of the word *die.*'

Jake blinked. 'And how many *have* been ... lost?' he spluttered.

Wilkinson smiled. 'Rest assured, I've had a one hundred per cent survival rate of all the Undoers I've handled thus far.'

Cora frowned. 'And how many Undoers have you handled?'

Wilkinson clapped his hands together excitedly. 'You're my first two. I only died a week ago. Exciting, isn't it. I'm sure we'll be a great team.'

He picked up the old-fashioned telephone and spoke into the handset.

'Hello? Oh, wrong line. Haha! Let's try again ...' He pressed another number. 'That's the one. Yes, hello. Maureen? Could you ask Bad Penny to take them home now, and stand down.'

He placed the handset back and smiled across the desk at them both.

'I really have no idea what I'm doing!'

Jake was just about to go and find the Ambassador, and return the box and the file and everything, and promptly hand in his resignation when, a hundred or so miles away, a bucket of cold water was thrown over his face.

The shock of this caused his spirit to whip across the ether and snap back into his body in the old shed in his dad's garden.

Bad Penny's special technique.

She peered at him as he wiped the slimy water from his face.

'So? You found out what you need to do?'

Jake nodded, pushing the sodden hair from his eyes.

'Good,' she huffed. She walked over to the table where she'd put Cora's trophy and flipped the lid closed. 'This will pull her back.'

Turning on her heels, she marched out of the shed.

Then she marched back in again and picked up the flask of tea she'd forgotten and marched out once more.

Jake looked at his feet. On the ground before him were the box and the book and the bundle of, now slightly soggy, papers. The black card was in his back pocket. He looked at it, turning it slightly, so that it caught the light. In shiny black letters on a matte black background was the word 'Wormling'. He groaned and put the card back in his pocket. He shook off the papers and looked at them again.

We believe that the emotional trauma of the betrayal has caused his haunting.

Jake remembered the wonderful feeling when he'd realised that Stiffkey, his spectral undertaker friend, had been trapped on the Earthly Plane because he'd never told his son that he loved him, and the joy on Stiffkey's face when, on shouting it out, his body had begun to fade.

Maybe he could do the same for Errol Clay? And suddenly, despite the stagnant water dripping down his face, Jake had to admit he was a little bit excited. The mission they'd been set didn't seem *too* dangerous. There'd be problems, of course. But it felt good to be doing good. They were going to help someone. Jake felt strangely elated.

A knocking sound came from the table and he remembered with a start that Cora was still inside the trophy. He opened the lid and she appeared.

Jake turned to face Cora, and said with purpose, 'There's no time to lose. We've got a ghost to Undo!'

The mood was slightly ruined by her reply.

'You've got a dead frog in your hair, Wormling.'

PORTENTIA

ortentia held her hand up and the door
swung open, propelled by the unseen force
of her mind. The use of Old Magic for such
things was strictly forbidden by the Embassy, but
she was a busy woman. She had no time to break
pace for a mere door.

At the end of the corridor, she turned into a
small room, and stood by the window, waiting. She
reached into the pocket of her long coat and pulled
out a pack of tarot cards, spinning them round in
the long and impeccably manicured fingers of her
left hand. She flipped the top card over with a twist
of her index finger and thumb.

On the card was a picture of a man in robes, a
wand in one hand pointing to the heavens, the other
pointing to the ground.

The Magician.

She gazed from the window. Outside, the hills of the moor could be seen stretching into the distance above the trees that surrounded the Embassy.

'Hello,' she said, not turning around.

A voice spoke from behind her. 'Do we have anything to worry about?'

Portentia flipped a second card. A burning building, struck by lightning, bodies leaping from its high windows.

The Tower.

She frowned at the dark omen. A price always had to be paid. But never by her.

'No, I will be at the club to personally ensure the shipment's safe arrival,' said Portentia.

She turned a final card.

The Queen of Coins.

She smiled. Her favourite.

The voice from the shadows spoke once more.

'Good. There is something of particular beauty in this load. We wouldn't want it getting lost.'

A smile flicked across Portentia's lips.

'Something of particular beauty?' she whispered.

'A gift ...' said the voice. 'For you.' He paused. 'Assuming nothing goes wrong.'

Portentia nodded. 'It won't'.

The voice continued.

'And Clay? It would be unfortunate to let him pass to the Afterworld when he's been so useful.'

'Don't worry, I've given his case to the children. They don't stand a chance of Undoing him.'

She placed the cards back into her coat pocket and without saying goodbye walked past him out of the room.

SOUNDS LIKE TROUBLE

Mum frowned. 'You want to go to London, on your own?'

Jake nodded. 'Well, not on my own, with Sab,' Jake clarified. 'Sab's got tickets to go to a games expo for his birthday.'

It wasn't a lie. *Technically.* Sab's older cousin, Sammy, *had* bought him tickets for the expo for his birthday. And he had invited Sab and a friend of his choosing, and Sab had chosen Jake.

It didn't stop it feeling like a lie, though. Because Jake had other, much darker reasons for wanting to go to London.

Jake poured himself a bowl of cornflakes to distract from the silence. Then he started reading the back of the packet. Out loud. To try and sound relaxed.

'*A good source of vitamins and minerals*,' he said, in what he hoped was a nonchalant tone.

Mum's frowned deepened. 'You're behaving very strangely.' She paused. 'This is a computer games thing, right? Like a show?'

Jake nodded. 'A fair. There are loads of stands about new games and things.'

'Oh.'

'Oh' wasn't promising. Jake's mum hated *all* computer games. Which was weird. How can you hate *all* computer games? It's a bit like saying you hate *all* music. Or *all* books. It's not like she'd played *all* the computer games. It's not like she'd even played *one* computer game. As far as he knew, anyway.

It was time to bring out the sugar-coating.

'Sab's cousin is taking us.'

'Nice Sammy? Are you sure he doesn't mind?'

Mum liked Sab's cousin, 'nice' Sammy. Jake wasn't sure why. It might be because he was really polite and had been wearing a suit when she met him. Sammy was in his twenties. And he had a proper job that paid proper money. In fact, Jake was fairly sure he earned more money than his mum and dad put together, hence the free tickets.

'He said if we get the train, he can meet us at the station.'

'What did your dad say?'

'He said to ask you?'

'Typical.' Mum frowned again. Then she sighed, and walked out of the room. 'I'll phone Sammy and check it's not too much trouble.'

Jake had decided not to mention the fact that he'd be skipping out of the expo as soon as possible to track down the ghost of a former armed robber. It seemed like an unnecessary detail.

Cora appeared before him.

'Don't you think we should discuss this?' She had her hands on her hips. 'We haven't even worked out how to Undo Errol Clay yet! Please tell me you're not going to just turn up. You know how you crack under pressure.'

'I already know how we're going to Undo him,' said Jake smugly.

'How?' Cora looked unconvinced.

'I found something on the Internet.'

He held up his phone. Cora peered at it. Then she looked up at Jake.

'Very cute,' she said dryly.

Jake looked at the phone. He'd accidently opened an app that he'd used to superimpose bunny ears on a photo of himself.

'Oh! Hang on,' he said, reddening. He fiddled with his phone. 'I meant this one.'

'A book review for a book that came out two years ago?'

'Just read it!' urged Jake.

Cora began to read aloud.

'The Inside Man: The Autobiography of Detective Jonah Franks. *The brothers Ethan and Errol Clay need no introduction. For two decades their criminal enterprises held the Shabwell district of East London in a vice-like grip of extortion and violent crime.*'

She looked at Jake.

'Scroll.'

'Oh right, sorry,' said Jake. Cora's hands would go straight through the phone, so he had to do it for her. He scrolled down the page as she read on . . .

'The Inside Man *is the thrilling account of the*

undercover policeman who infiltrated their gang, and the crimes he witnessed.'

She looked at Jake again. 'Scroll.'

Jake scrolled down some more.

'Undercover cop, Jonah "The Whale" Franks rose to the rank of a trusted confidante of the brothers, until finally betraying them in the botched heist that became known as the Shabwell Square Job.'

Cora looked up expectantly. 'Scroll!' she said impatiently.

Jake could see why lacking a physical presence might get frustrating.

'The heist lead to the death of Errol Clay and the imprisonment of his older brother Ethan, but the stolen loot was never recovered . . .'

She stopped reading. 'Not as dumb as you look, Precious! It wasn't his own brother who betrayed him. It was Jonah Franks!'

Jake smiled smugly. 'Yup! We just show Errol Clay this book review, and abracadabra – he's Undone! Easy peasy!'

Cora frowned. 'A bit *too* easy if you ask me. Portentia's been working on the case for three months according to Wilkinson. It's hardly like this was difficult to find. I wonder why she didn't Undo him herself?'

Jake shrugged. 'Thanks for the vote of confidence. Maybe she doesn't have the initiative? Maybe she's too busy with other stuff? Like stopping the forces of Fenris plunging the Earthly Plane into an Age of Evil ... Little things like that.'

Cora looked thoughtful for a couple of seconds. She opened her mouth to say something, then paused as Mum walked in.

'On your phone again, Jake?' said Mum as he pocketed it. 'Who were you talking to?' She looked at him strangely.

'Oh, just Sab.'

Her eyes narrowed. 'Sab? You don't normally speak to Sab. You normally message Sab.'

She was right. She looked at him, taking care to catch his eye.

'Have you got a girlfriend?'

'Mum!' said Jake, feeling himself redden.

'Fat chance!' came Cora's laughing voice from behind his mum.

'OK, OK!' said Mum, breaking into a smile. She had that funny look she got in her eyes sometimes. Like she was going to cry with joy.

'My little boy's growing into a man. Going to London without his mummy!'

Jake cringed and she laughed, reaching across the table, and brushed his hair back away from his forehead.

'I'm so proud of you, Jake,' she said.

Not for the first time, Jake felt more than a little guilty.

SLIPPING AWAY

Jake was sitting in a toilet cubicle pretending to do a poo. The expo was so busy, he'd had to close Cora's trophy as soon as they'd arrived. There was always a chance that someone might see her. Someone like Jake: someone *sensitive*, who could see ghosts, but perhaps hadn't stumbled across one before. The last thing they needed was someone freaking out over the sight of a semi-transparent schoolgirl.

Jake wished Stiffkey was here now. Well, not literally *here*, inside the toilet cubicle. That would be weird. But he wished Stiffkey was around. He missed the old ghost, though it had to be said, meeting him had brought him a lot of trouble.

Jake flushed the toilet in case anyone was listening outside. He felt in his bag to make sure Cora's trophy was still safely stowed. He smiled.

It had brought him a friend too.

In fact, it had doubled his friend count. Now he had two. Cora and Sab. But it was weird when Cora and Sab were together, and the train ride to London had been no different. Sometimes Cora would make a joke that Jake couldn't react to for fear that Sab would think he was mad, or Sab would make a joke, but Jake would miss it, or Cora would reply first, and then the moment was gone. He felt like he was lying to his best friend, and he hated it. Jake had often thought about telling Sab about his ghostly friend. But telling an unlicensed member of the living about a ghost was forbidden by the Embassy. And besides, the words of Stiffkey often popped into his head, as though the old undertaker was still keeping an eye on them somehow:

No good ever comes of the living meeting the dead.

Cora had agreed never to take advantage of Sab's insensitivity to ghosts. And for someone who enjoyed playing pranks on people as much as she did, that was difficult for her, to say the least.

Instead she contented herself with dramatic eye-rolling at Sab and Jake's conversations.

Jake and Cora's friendship was very similar to his and Sab's in that they never really talked about feelings and stuff – they spent most of their time joking around – but Jake often found himself wondering about Cora. She was different to Sab. If Sab's life was an open book, Cora's had every third chapter ripped out.

She'd said once that she didn't like her parents and certainly, when she'd been freed from her trophy, she had only ever wanted to come home with Jake, not go back to her home, wherever that had been. Jake had never asked her why, or mentioned it since. It wasn't that he didn't care. He just didn't know how. You can't force people to talk about their problems. You have to let them do it in their own time. He should really let her know that he was there for her, if she ever wanted to discuss anything. But that was easier said than done with Cora.

Most of the time she seemed quite content pestering Jake, making fun of him and Sab. Just once though, when Jake and Sab had been laughing and playing computer games, he'd caught a strange look pass across her face, one he didn't often see on Cora. She'd looked sad. Jake was used to only having one or (counting the dead) two friends, but it must be hard for her, he thought. At school she'd almost been Head Girl. He could imagine her surrounded by underlings, hanging off her every word. Now she just had him and a ghost fox.

Zorro had come with them to London, of course. Jake and Cora had tried to leave Zorro behind for this trip, encouraging him to roam the countryside surrounding the farm for a couple of days – after all, it's not like he needed feeding. It was easier said than done. The ghost fox followed them around like a shadow, never wanting to stray far from their side for more than a few minutes. To be honest, Jake was often glad of his company. He'd grown fond of the funny little creature, even if he was a bit needy. The fox looked up at him now as if to say, *Are you going to be much longer?*

Jake had needed a plan to get away from Sab for an hour or so whilst at the exhibition so he and Cora could go and find Errol's snooker club. But nothing he came up with seemed to convince Sab.

'I think I'll watch another demonstration instead of the *WarCry3* one,' Jake had said on the train down, faking a thoughtful expression as he looked through the programme.

Sab looked at Jake incredulously. 'What could be better than the *WarCry3* launch?'

Jake hadn't thought that far ahead. He cursed inwardly and casually glanced at the page of events that he had open in front of him. There was only one that clashed with *WarCry3*.

'*Pony Club Manager*?' he tried.

Sab laughed. 'Ha ha, very funny!'

Cora's head poked through the seat and she rolled her eyes at Jake. 'Idiot.'

The fake poo was Plan B. Jake knew the crowds for the *WarCry* launch would be huge. His plan was to sit here so long that Sab would be forced to go in without him. Then Jake would tell him it was too full and he'd watch it from the back and meet him after. That would give him one hour exactly to do what he needed to do and be back for lunch. It was *foolproof*.

Right on time, his phone beeped. It was Sab.

Where are you? It's warcry3 time!!!! I'm inside. Front Left. It's rammed!

Jake tapped out his reply.

I'm still queuing. I'll find a space at the back. See you after at the Burger Stand.

K

And just like that – the plan was in action.

He pulled his trousers up and opened the cubicle door. He'd better get a move on. Cora did not enjoy being trapped in her trophy. He snuck from the toilets, checking left and right to make sure the coast was clear, then he pulled his hood up over his head and snuck off towards the exit, Zorro trotting along at his heels.

Like he'd said – *foolproof!*

FINDING ERROL CLAY

I t was hard to believe how much a city could change after just a few stops on the Underground.

The stop for the games expo had been clean and corporate. A teeming crowd of gamers old and young had surged from the train, up a shining escalator to be shepherded by flashing signs and polo-shirted guides, straight into the massive entrance of the Expo Centre, a sensory overload of lights and sounds. The Shabwell Docks stop was *very* different. Jake was the only one to disembark, and there were no escalators, just a short flight of dirty stairs, through the ticket barriers, and out on to a street shadowed by large brick warehouses. As Jake walked along the road, he caught occasional glimpses of the huge, murky river that snaked through the city. It felt exciting to be here in this vast, anonymous place, so different to the sleepy little village where he was from.

He went through a mental checklist of his achievements so far.

He'd worked out how to Undo Errol Clay.

He'd got to London on his own.

He'd snuck out of the expo unseen by Sab.

Everything was going to plan. Maybe he wasn't such a bad Undoer after all? A few hundred metres later, he checked his phone and realised he'd been walking in completely the wrong direction.

He turned around and went back the way he'd come. After he passed the Tube stop again, he double-checked his phone and turned into an alley. Walking a safe distance from the entrance, he squatted down and opened his bag. Then he carefully lifted the lid of Cora's trophy, replacing the piece of string he kept taped to the inside of the lid in order to make sure it stayed open.

He looked around for her.

Cora was nowhere to be seen. 'Cora?' he hissed. 'Where are you?'

'Boo!' He felt a hard hockey-stick-like prod in his back and he tumbled forward from his squatting position on to his knees on the wet ground.

'Really? Is that appropriate behaviour for an Undoer's assistant?'

Cora was leaning on her stick, chuckling. 'Undoer's *partner.* If anything, as the older and more educated one of the team, I should really be in charge.'

She looked down at Jake, sprawling in the gutter. 'I'm not sure you've got the leadership qualities, to be frank.'

Jake considered closing the lid of her trophy again, but instead stood up and slung his rucksack on his back. Then, flicking dirt from his trousers, he started walking down the alleyway. He waved his phone at her.

'Unfortunately for you, I've got the map so I guess *I'm* the one in the lead.'

The map led Jake and Cora away from the alley they were in and down another one that opened up on to the banks of the river. In the distance Jake could see the gleaming towers and shiny skyscrapers of the city. The district they were in was quite different. An almost deserted path, wet with rain, followed the river for a while, then bent away from it to make room for a row of huge brick warehouses butted up against the water.

They turned into another alleyway that led them between the warehouses and to a small square. Around the square were small workshops. Inside one of them – a garage – a mechanic was looking into the open bonnet of a car. His eyes followed Jake as he walked across the square.

There, on the other side, was the former site of Clay's Snooker Club. Now it seemed to be being used as some kind of storage facility. It also seemed to be completely closed. Definitely not the sort of place you walk up to the front door of and ring the bell.

'Let's see if there's a side entrance,' said Jake, keen to get away from the mechanic's watchful gaze. They headed down the footpath that ran alongside the warehouse.

The mechanic watched Jake go. It was unusual to see a child on their own in this part of Shabwell. He could've sworn that just for a split second he'd seen a girl too, with some funny-looking dog slinking round her ankles, but when he'd looked back they had both disappeared, and it was just the boy, alone. He scratched his head. Must be seeing things.

The mechanic tried to carry on with his work, but something kept drawing his eyes back to the deserted old snooker club. He blinked as again something strange flickered into view – a face looking out from one of the tiny grimy windows of the warehouse, pressed up against the glass; a scowling, brooding face staring murder out over the square. The mechanic blinked again and the face was gone. He rubbed his eyes and opened them again. No, nothing there. It must have been a trick of the light. He chuckled to himself as he picked up his tools and got back to work again.

'Definitely seeing things . . .' he muttered.

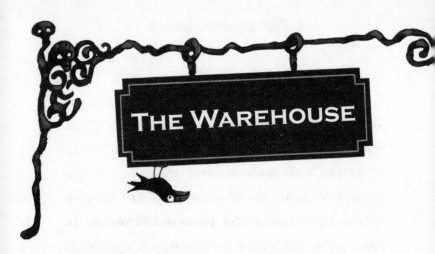

THE WAREHOUSE

Having a friend that can push her face through solid brick walls has its advantages. *Sometimes.*

'I can't see anything. It's pitch black in there.'

They were standing by some bins on a footpath that led alongside the old snooker club, next to a rusty iron fire escape that climbed, three storeys, to a metal door. Zorro was rooting around quite happily behind the bins. Jake and Cora stood at the bottom of the steps, looking up. It didn't look like the staircase had been used in a long time. In fact, several treads were missing and the whole structure seemed to be pulling away from the wall.

'We'll have to try round the back,' said Jake. 'I'm not climbing that. It looks like it was built in the Stone Age!'

Cora sighed and pushed past him. 'Unfunny and factually inaccurate – if it was built in the Stone Age, it would have been made of stone and these stairs are clearly made from metal.'

She stomped soundlessly up the stairs, skipping over a missed step and pausing halfway up to pirouette gracefully. She took an overly dramatic bow.

'It's perfectly safe, Precious!'

'It's all right for you. You're already dead!' Jake put his foot on the first step and felt the entire structure wobble. 'And ghosts probably don't weigh anything.'

Jake slowly began to ascend the stairs, sure with every step that the whole structure would collapse. But to his relief it held together. At the top, the stairs opened out on to a small landing and a door leading back into the building.

The door, of course, was locked, but Cora walked through it anyway.

Jake heard a bang and the door swung open. Cora was standing on the other side, holding up her hockey stick triumphantly.

'A fire door, thankfully! I just pushed on the bar with my hockey stick, and it opened!'

Jake stepped inside. A corridor ran left and right. He looked at Cora. 'Which way shall we go?'

Cora looked back at him. 'We?' she said, seating herself smugly on the steps.

Jake frowned for a second, then remembered why Undoers were always the living, not the dead. According to Bad Penny, the presence of an Undoer's ghost makes the Undoing that much more difficult. What was it she had said? Something about how other ghosts' 'energies' confuse things.

'Right then,' sighed Jake. 'I guess I'm on my own then.' He had started walking off when Cora called him back.

'Aren't you forgetting something?' she said.

He blinked, then realised he still had his rucksack on with Cora's trophy in it. He took it off and placed it on the steps next to her.

Cora shook her head. 'So ironic that the cowardly one has to do all the scary stuff.'

Jake looked left then right down the corridor. Right looked slightly less forbidding. 'I choose right.'

'Good luck, Precious. I'll wait for you here.'

It wasn't the first time Jake had been alone in an empty building looking for a ghost, but if he was honest, it was the sort of thing he'd never get totally used to. He could feel his heart thumping, and the familiar fear creeping through his body with every step he took into the darkness.

The corridor turned to the right. Now the ceiling was punctuated with skylights and Jake could see his feet making prints in the thick layer of dust. He pulled his hoodie up over his nose, conscious of not wanting to breathe it in.

At the end of the corridor he reached a door and slowly pushed it open. Suddenly he was on an open metal walkway running over the cavernous warehouse space below. Looking down he could see it was filled with neat avenues of wooden crates. He wondered where all the snooker tables were now. With every step he took, the walkway creaked under his feet, echoing around the empty space. His heart was pumping faster as he made his way towards the door at the end of the walkway, trying to keep his movements as quiet as possible.

He didn't even know why he was heading for this door in particular, but something seemed to be guiding his steps. Despite the pounding of his heart, he didn't doubt where he was going. One step at a time, he made his way along the walkway until he reached the door at the other side of the building. He pushed it open gingerly and stepped through into a messy office – papers littering a desk and a half-drunk cup of coffee, lit up by light streaming through a large dirty window that overlooked the river.

'Hello?' he said, hearing his voice breaking with nerves. 'Mr Clay?'

There was no answer. He felt stupid now. Did he expect the ghost would just come at his call?

He looked around the office. It seemed fairly unremarkable, except for the mess and the fact that it could do with a good lick of paint. For some reason Jake's eyes settled on some dark rust-coloured spots on the wall below the window, just above an old-fashioned radiator. He felt a chill go through him, though he was unsure why.

He wandered over to the spots on the wall and

crouched down to inspect them – one larger and two smaller ones. To many people they would appear to be damp spots, perhaps, or dismissed as ancient stains. To Jake, though, they were something else, something much more sinister. He pressed his thumb on to the larger spot, and stretched his fingers to reach the two smaller spots. They fell short, but it was enough to convince him – these were fingerprints, and they were made in blood.

A sudden pain shot thorough his head and he shut his eyes. In his mind, he could see the office. But now it was tidy. Now it was someone else's office. Someone else's office from a long time ago. Now a brighter sun shone through a cleaner window. He spun round as the door was opened and a shaven-headed man stumbled through. One hand was holding a brown leather bag, and the other was pressed to his side, stemming the flow of blood that was seeping from an open wound, staining his white shirt with crimson. He had no awareness that Jake was in the room, and Jake realised that this was because he wasn't. He was watching something that had happened years ago. He'd had this type of vision once before, when he'd witnessed the murder of Zorro's owner. When it had happened then he was hardly aware it was a vision. This time he knew he was seeing something that wasn't there. Something that had happened a long time ago.

The man grimaced in pain and swung the door shut behind him. He staggered towards Jake and knelt by the wall, reaching behind the radiator for something. He moved his other hand from his wound, steadying himself against the wall, his bloodied fingers leaving the marks that time would soon fade to three small brown blotches. There was a click and a floorboard moved enough to allow the man to get his fingers underneath. Lifting it, he shifted the leather bag into the gap beneath the floorboards, then shoved the bag right down and away from the hole before replacing the floorboard. Then he stood up, a grim smile on his face. Leaning over his desk, he scrabbled for the drawer at the front, and it was half open when shouting came from outside. Shouting from a distant time. 'You might as well give up, Clay! Come quietly so no one else gets hurt.'

The man looked up from the desk, shut the half-opened drawer, and sighed. Jake could see a look of anguish on his face. Tears pouring from his eyes. He pulled himself up straight and, beating his chest with his hands, he lifted his head and roared like a cornered beast.

Jake's eyes flicked open. He was on the floor of the messy office, lying on his back, blinking up at the ceiling.

'So this is where it happened,' he muttered to himself.

A voice spoke. 'Yeah it is. And what are you doing lying on my carpet?'

Jake sat up. Sitting on the desk of the office was a semi-transparent form of the shaven-headed man from Jake's vision – his head set low on huge shoulders, his white shirt still stained with the blood from his fatal wound.

It was the ghost of Errol Clay.

ERROL CLAY

'Dunno what the world's comin' to when even kids come lookin' for me loot.'

Errol Clay cracked his knuckles.

Jake remembered the book review . . .

The stolen money was never found.

He scratched his head. The thought of retrieving the money for himself hadn't even crossed his mind. *Idiot.*

Errol Clay shrugged. 'Takes all sorts, I suppose.'

'I-I'm not here for your money,' said Jake.

Clay's eyes narrowed. 'Can you see me then, boy?' he snarled. 'Is that it? You one of those sensitive types?' The ghost of Errol Clay knelt beside Jake and pressed his big face right up against Jake's until Jake felt the coldness of the man's semi-transparent nose overlapping with his own. 'Can you give me a reason why I shouldn't throw you out the window?'

'Yes, I can,' said Jake as confidently as he could muster. His hand gripped his phone. Saved on the screen was the newspaper article. The article that would Undo Errol Clay. He cleared his throat. 'I'm from the Embassy of the Dead,' he said, 'and I'm here to Undo you.'

Errol Clay laughed. He looked around the room as though he was expecting others to be there.

'Can't believe they sent a kid! Where's the lady?'

Jake paused. 'Portentia?'

Errol Clay nodded. 'That's the one. She's a bit easier on the eye than you, that's for sure.'

Jake frowned. It seemed odd that Portentia would have met Errol Clay before. Surely she would have Undone him herself.

'I'm handling your case now.' Jake was surprised by the calmness of his own voice.

Errol Clay looked out of the window across the Thames. He sounded suspicious. 'If an adult can't help me then how can a kid? Portentia said it was impossible. Barely even tried.'

'Well –' Jake swallowed, suddenly nervous – 'I have information here that will allow you to pass to the Afterworld.'

'There is nothing on God's earth that will let me pass,' growled Clay. He spun round angrily. 'You ever been betrayed? By your own flesh and blood? I ain't got time for this.' His lip curled into a snarl. 'Ain't nothing that can heal this broken heart. Cos that's what's keeping me here.' He banged a massive fist against his chest. 'It's the only thing I can feel through the pain of the longings.'

Jake held up his phone, determined to help him.

'That's the thing. You weren't betrayed by your brother . . . It's all here.'

Errol Clay's eyes narrowed.

'Show me,' he croaked, reaching out for the phone. But as he started reading he seemed to change his mind. 'No. I . . . I can't, it's too much . . . you read it to me,' he said, shoving the phone at Jake and shutting his eyes tight against the tears.

Jake took back his phone and, swallowing an uncomfortable lump in his throat, slowly began to read the article out loud.

'Undercover cop, Jonah "The Whale" Franks, rose to the rank of a trusted confidante of the brothers, until –' Jake looked up at Errol, who was wiping away tears as Jake said the words that he hoped would Undo him – *'finally betraying them in the botched heist that became known as the Shabwell Square Job.'*

Errol Clay opened his eyes wide, then blinked. At first he seemed incredulous. 'He was a *cop*!?' He frowned and shook his head in disbelief. 'Why, I'd have ripped his arms off if I'd known—' He fell silent.

Jake looked at him and Clay looked back.

'Oh Ethan,' he said, his voice beginning to crack again. His hand reached out towards Jake, as though Jake was his brother. 'I'm sorry, Ethan ...'

He staggered slightly then stood up taller, and smiled. Now the tears were streaming down his cheeks. 'I knew it couldn't be so ... In my heart I knew he weren't no snitch ...'

He looked down at his hands, and back up at Jake in disbelief. They were fading! 'I'm moving on!' There was an expression of pure joy on his face

- almost childlike - and Jake too felt a deep sense of happiness, that some great wrong in the world had been righted.

Then something changed on Clay's face. 'Listen,' he said, 'I gotta tell you, I gotta confess . . . Make my peace . . .' His face looked desperate suddenly, and Jake felt a chill pass right through him. 'I been working with her, smuggling stuff . . .'

'What?' stammered Jake. 'With who?' He was finding it hard to come out of the rapturous joy he'd been feeling only moments before. *Smuggling?* His mind shot back to the briefing room. To the words he and Cora had heard Portentia say about the missing ghost, Amber Chase.

It seems she got a little bit too involved with the smugglers.

'Something bad's coming . . . and coming soon . . . you gotta get there, stop it . . .'

Jake had turned white. 'Get where?'

Errol Clay had all but disappeared now, little more than a shimmer in the air, but with a last flick of his hand he pulled something from his pocket and chucked it at Jake.

'Thank you!' he said.

And with that, Errol Clay disappeared.

Jake was in a state of shock. He'd gone from high to low to high again in the space of a few minutes and, quite frankly, he had no idea if he was coming or going.

He looked down at the floor to where whatever it was Errol had thrown at him had fluttered to the ground. He almost didn't want to pick it up. What if he *didn't*? What if he never had to find out?

I've been working with her ... smuggling things ... something bad's coming ...

Could he be talking about the missing pilot, Amber Chase? Had he been working with her?

Jake bent down and picked up what had been thrown at him. It was a book of tickets. Flicking through it he saw that there were seven empty ticket stubs and three remaining tickets.

The tickets were empty of any information, apart from a crude drawing of a dead tree with an evil-looking bird roosting in a dead tree. As Jake studied the image, some words formed from nowhere written within the branches of the tree:

The Hangman's Club,
Albemarle Street,
Opens Midnight

'Is it done?' said Cora suddenly appearing in the doorway. 'Or should I say, is *he* Undone?'

Jake nodded, slipping the tickets in his pockets. 'Yup!' he said. 'It's finished. Over. Definitely nothing else to do.'

Cora narrowed her eyes suspiciously. She looked him up and down. 'What's that in your pocket?' she asked.

'Nothing,' said Jake. He just needed a minute to think . . .

'Is there something you're not telling me, Precious?'

Everything in Jake's body was telling him to ignore *everything* that Errol Clay had told him. About Amber and the smugglers and the

Hangman's Club.

It wasn't his problem. And to be honest, it all sounded quite dangerous. They should quit while they were ahead.

And yet . . . he couldn't just do nothing. Could he?

Something bad's coming . . .

Jake sighed deeply. 'I think I know where she is,' he muttered.

'Who?'

'The girl the Embassy are looking for. The pilot. Amber Chase.'

Jake reached into his pocket and pulled out the tickets, passing them to Cora.

Cora's eyes lit up like fireworks. 'Then what are we waiting for, Precious?'

Jake looked at her and couldn't help smiling.

'Well, I guess we're waiting until midnight for the Hangman's Club to open, aren't we?'

STICKMEN

Jake lay awake, fully dressed, in a sleeping bag on the floor of Sammy's flat, listening to the sound of Sab snoring. It had been a long day, but for Jake it wasn't over yet.

He'd made it back in time for lunch in the conference hall canteen where Jake had had to bluff his way through a conversation with a very excited Sab about *WarCry3*. To be honest, Sab was so excited, Jake could have said 'I just helped a ghost pass to the Afterworld whose dying wish was for me to save the Earthly Plane from a nefarious smuggling plot ...' and Sab probably wouldn't have even heard him. He'd got away with it anyway, and Sammy had paid for the burgers, which was just as well when a burger and fries cost nearly £15.

'That's London for you,' said Sammy, getting his wallet out.

Sab and Jake had hung out together in the afternoon and they'd chatted happily as they'd wandered round all the demo stands looking for new games. Jake himself was a bit preoccupied by his forthcoming evening mission, but Sab didn't seem to notice.

Jake looked at his phone, shielding the glow with his sleeping bag.

23.31 . . .

He lay still, listening to Sab's breathing, then quietly as he could, he pulled his clothes and shoes on, stepped into the hallway, nodded at Cora, who was sitting on the stairs reading **THE BOOK OF THE DEAD**, and crept out through the front door.

It was cold outside and Jake wished he'd brought his thick winter coat. 'Where's Zorro?' he said, looking around, shivering.

'Where do you think?'

Jake looked down the street. Outside every house, shining under the streetlights, was a pile of black bin bags.

Jake whistled softly and Zorro's head appeared from behind one of the piles.

'C'mon boy!' He watched as Zorro loped across the road and, together, the living boy, a ghost girl and a dead fox made their way to the end of the street where Jake had found out that a night bus would pass on its way to Albemarle Street.

It was raining now. The type of rain that seemed to be dirty before it even hit the streets.

Jake's finger tapped nervously on the seat in front of him. 'Do you think we should let Wilkinson know?' he asked Cora. In his rucksack was the Necrommunicator - or the Mousephone as he and Cora preferred to call it. All he had to do was press the button inside, and they could let Wilkinson know that they had a lead in the Amber Chase case.

Cora pulled a face. 'Don't be a simpleton. Firstly, we don't even know she's going to be at the Hangman's Club. Secondly, we're not even supposed to know about her. It will be obvious we spied on a secret meeting. Thirdly, they'll give *our information* to a more qualified Undoer to take care of it, and I didn't get to where I am today by letting other people take the credit for my triumphs!'

'And where are you today exactly?' asked Jake.

'On my way to the adventure of a lifetime! With VIP tickets to an exclusive ghostly hang out, on a mission to save the world – again!'

'I'm just worried we're getting into something that's a bit ... dangerous?' he finished lamely.

Cora looked at him sympathetically. 'Don't worry, Precious, I'll look after you ... We just need to get there, see if she's there, and what she's planning on smuggling, then we'll let the Embassy know. Best of both worlds.'

Jake nodded. It made sense. Pretty much everything Cora said made sense. It was one of her more annoying traits.

A road sign flashed by through the window of the bus. *Albemarle Street.*

'We're here,' said Jake, wishing they weren't. He rang the bell and the night bus pulled up at the end of the street that supposedly held the location of the mysterious Hangman's Club.

Jake and Cora, with Zorro right behind, hopped off the bus on to a wide street lined with identically grand town houses – each five storeys high with steps up to the front doors. Definitely not the kind of street you would think to find a place known as the Hangman's Club, Jake thought, but what would he know?

The street was dimly lit, street lamps providing just enough light to catch the rain as it fell against the pavement. The snow had completely melted now, but it was still cold, and Jake again regretted not bringing a proper coat. He looked across at Cora, but however cold he was, he still didn't envy the fact that she couldn't feel it. Feeling things was part of being alive . . . And she was . . . well, dead.

Jake paused and scratched his head. 'How do we know which house it's in?'

'Wait,' said Cora, stopping dead. 'Can you hear that music?' she asked.

'What?' said Jake.

'That music . . .'

Ahead of them, Zorro too had paused, his body alert and head cocked to one side, listening.

Jake caught up to him and crouched down, stroking his head, feeling the familiar slight resistance of Zorro's fur against his hand.

'What is it, Zorro?'

Cora laughed. 'You still can't hear it? And you're supposed to be sensitive!'

Jake stopped dead still to listen, straining his ears as hard as he could. At first it sounded like a far-off party, or a festival, distorted music carried and broken by the breeze, delivered to his ears in waves. Then as he concentrated, the music began to form into recognisable melodies – getting louder and louder, a fast, swinging rhythm, punctuated by yelps, shouting and laughter.

'Where is it coming from?' Jake looked around the empty street. The house he was standing in front of looked identical to all the others.

Cora's eyes seemed to settle on something and she looked up at Jake and laughed. 'Seems you're not as sensitive as you might like to think.'

She tapped her hockey stick on the pavement.

Jake couldn't be sure if the chalk-scrawled picture had been there before and he just hadn't been looking for it, or if it had only just appeared to him, like a ghost appearing from thin air.

It was a drawing that on first glance might have been done by a five-year-old child. A drawing of a tree, scratched in chalky lines across the paving stone in front of them.

Jake felt for the tickets, pulling them from his pocket.

'Look!' he whispered. 'The same!'

Except ...

Jake swallowed hard. The childlike drawing on the paving stone seemed to have changed and grown. Jake could now see ropes hanging down from the branches, and from the ropes hung sinister-looking stickmen. And for a second it looked like they moved, swinging in an imperceptible breeze.

And as Cora and Jake watched, half amazed, half horrified, again the picture changed and the branches began to grow and grow, spreading now like a crack in the pavement, zigzagging chalk lines splintering up stone steps, branching and twisting and extending, until they reached the top of the steps, ending in front of a large black door, at which point the door creaked slowly open.

Cora looked at Jake and raised an eyebrow.

'Do you think this is the place then?' she asked dryly, and before Jake could stop her, she had shot up the steps and slipped inside.

Portentia stepped out from the shadows of Albemarle Street, a long coat wrapped around her, protecting her from the cold night. She reached into her pocket and took out a phone.

The person at the other end answered, and said nothing. Just waited for her to speak.

'We have a problem,' she said. 'The Wormling is here. He must know something.'

'How could he know? Can you get to him?'

'They've gone in. How far away are you?'

'Not far,' he said. 'Don't worry. Our shadowy friends are preparing to strike. They'll deal with the boy. And his assistant. And yours.'

There was a pause. 'What shall I do?'

'Wait for me outside. We can't risk you going in till all threats are neutralised. Leave it to the shadows . . .'

'Very well,' she said, and hung up. Portentia reached into her pocket and pulled out her pack of cards.

She looked up at the Hangman's Club. From outside it looked like all the other houses on the street. A patch of darkness flashed across her vision, as though a cloud had moved across a moonlit sky. The Shadowfolk had already begun to arrive.

She flipped over the top card.

Death.

Yes, probably best to wait outside.

IF YOUR NAME'S NOT DOWN . . .

The door to the Hangman's Club opened up into a small entrance, dominated by a huge, turbaned man standing before Jake and Cora with his arms crossed and a face like thunder.

They looked up at him, waiting for him to speak.

A few seconds passed. Jake shifted uncomfortably from foot to foot as the man glared down at them.

He pointed at Zorro. 'No animals.'

He pointed at Jake and Cora. 'No children.'

He pointed at Jake again. 'AND DEFINITELY NO LIVING.'

Then he proceeded to look right past them as if they were no longer there.

Jake fumbled in his pockets. 'We, um, we have these . . .' he stammered, taking out the tickets and handing them to the man.

The man looked at the tickets. 'Ah!' His face crinkled into a surprisingly friendly smile. 'Why didn't you say?' He bowed deep. 'You may enter . . .' He clapped his hands and the door behind him opened, with a blast of music, and laughter.

Jake nodded a polite *thank you* as he squeezed past the man's massive body, and Cora followed close behind, giving the man a withering look as she walked past, muttering, 'Don't you know who I am?' under her breath.

The door opened into a crowded room. It was like the weirdest house party ever. Jake groaned inwardly. He wasn't the biggest fan of parties. Not that he got invited to many having just the one living friend, Sab. He wished Sab was here. Sab would have actually enjoyed this party. It was like a crazy fancy dress party – except if none of the guests realised they were in fancy dress.

Jake squeezed through a group of young men with white hair and blood-spattered suits sitting around on a sofa. One of them, not much older than Jake himself, looked at him and nodded.

Cora too was taking in the assorted crowd. 'I wonder what happened to them? And . . . oh my!'

Jake looked up. It wasn't often Cora was lost for words.

A ballerina in a battered swan costume tottered down the grand staircase. A passing man with a tremendous moustache, noticing Jake's dropped jaw as he took in the ballerina, stooped to whisper in Jake's ear in an unrecognisable accent, 'The great Irena Mueller. Was crushed by a falling sandbag live on stage in Berlin, apparently.' He chuckled. 'What a way to go!'

The ballerina paused on the stairs to let Zorro trot past and a look of disgust flashed across her face at the sight of the animal. She composed herself and continued down the stairs.

'Cora!' hissed Jake. 'Zorro's gone upstairs!'

Cora shrugged. 'We've got a job to do. We've got to find Amber Chase . . . Who knows, maybe Zorro's looking too.'

Jake nodded, and peered around the room. On the one hand, it was a terrifying place to find yourself, alone at midnight, and yet on the other hand, he had to admit he felt strangely . . . at home. Accepted, almost. No one was giving him a second look. That was the thing with ghosts, he supposed. Stiffkey had said that spirits were trapped on the Earthly Plane as a result of trauma suffered around the time of death. It seemed to Jake, looking around, that anybody, no matter who they had been or how they had died, could suffer the bad luck of becoming a ghost. It was a mixed crowd. And one thing was obvious – these unlikely party guests bound together by the misfortune of their shared longings liked to party.

With the sound of a needle being clumsily lifted from a record, the music stopped suddenly to be replaced almost instantly by the sound of someone breaking into spontaneous song. It was the strangely accented voice of the moustachioed man singing words that Jake didn't understand.

Cora stood on a chair and peered over the packed crowd of ghostly guests.

'Any sign of a pilot?' asked Jake.

She jumped down. 'No, but there's a nearly-naked lady holding a boa constrictor, which is pretty cool.'

Jake sighed. Maybe Clay *was* just ranting? It didn't look like anything very sinister was going on – just a load of ghosts having fun. Amber Chase probably wasn't even here. What would she be doing at a club like this when she was on the run anyway? For that matter, what was *he* doing in a club like this?

Just as Jake was about to suggest they leave, something caught his eye. A hand holding a cocktail glass safely above the gathered crowd, gracefully dancing its way across the room. Something about that cocktail glass reminded him of someone . . .

A glimpse of a face through the crowd confirmed it. It was Eustace: the Bodyshifter cloakroom attendant from the Embassy of the Dead! He would know what was going on here, surely.

Jake followed him through the crowd, trying to catch up. He seemed to be very popular and, to the people he met that all slapped his back, shared a joke, and kissed his cheek, it would have seemed that he had not a care in the world. But Jake could see something different. Jake could see Eustace glancing over people's shoulders whilst they spoke; he could see him looking around. He seemed nervous. Preoccupied. He was looking for something. *Or someone.*

Jake paused to allow a top-hatted gentleman to squeeze past. For a second he lost sight of Eustace and then, as Jake felt a sudden burst of cold night air on his face, he realised – the party had spilt out of the back door, behind the house.

Maybe Eustace was outside, he thought, and pressed his way through the crowd again, indicating to Cora to follow him. She was holding a sausage roll and sniffing it.

'What are you doing?' he asked.

Cora looked at him excitedly. 'I can smell it!' She took a small bite. 'And I can eat it! I can taste it! It's *so* good.' She stuffed the rest into her mouth.

Jake watched, unimpressed, as she wolfed down the sausage roll and grabbed another from a passing waiter.

She shrugged. 'I haven't eaten since 1990, so . . .' She crammed the second sausage roll into her mouth and reached for a third. 'I didn't even know ghosts *had* food!'

The waiter overheard. 'Oh, this food isn't ghost food, Miss . . . this food is from the Afterworld.'

Jake blinked. 'From the Afterworld? How do you . . .'

The waiter winked. 'Ask no questions . . . ' he said, and sauntered on.

Jake's mind was racing. Food from the Afterworld, brought to the Earthly Plane? Surely that wasn't allowed? And if they were smuggling food over . . .

'Come on,' said Jake, pushing through the crowd with renewed purpose. 'We need to talk to Eustace.'

'Who's Eustace?' said Cora.

'Someone who might be able to help us. He's in the back garden.'

At last he made it to the back door and stepped through.

The garden was much, much larger than Jake was expecting it to be – much larger than a garden in the middle of a residential city street *should* be. A path lit with candles wound its way through rows and rows of bushes and small trees, between which groups of ghosts were gathered, chatting merrily. It seemed to go on for miles, stretching back and back until it disappeared into the darkness beyond. In fact, now that he thought of it, *all* traces of the rest of the street had disappeared. There were no lights from neighbouring houses, no distant tower blocks, or skyscrapers – just the sight and sound of ghosts chatting by candlelight, as far as the darkness allowed.

And there, moving between the groups, cocktail in hand, was Eustace. Jake rushed over to him, Cora following close behind, and tapped him on the shoulder.

Eustace turned and blinked, taking a moment to place him. 'Goodness me – Jake! What a surprise to see you here. And you've brought a date? How charming!'

Jake blushed. 'She's not my—'

Eustace interrupted, leaning forward and whispering urgently, 'You shouldn't be here!'

He looked like he was about to go, then stopped suddenly as a huddle of laughing ghosts stumbled past. Straightening up, he put his arm around Cora's shoulder. 'I love your little hat by the way, wherever did you get it?'

He walked them down the path to a quiet spot beneath a tree, where they couldn't be overheard.

'You must leave!' he whispered urgently. 'This is no place for children. There are bad people here . . .'

Cora looked straight at Eustace. 'We're actually here on Embassy business. We heard that the missing pilot had been seen here, at the Hangman's Club. We know she's involved in a smuggling plot, and we've come to find her for the Embassy.'

Eustace rolled his eyes. 'Really now? You clearly have no idea what's going on.'

Jake lowered his voice. 'We know she's a smuggler.'

Eustace shook his head. 'If you knew Amber, you would know she'd never do anything like that. She's here looking for . . .' He fell silent.

Cora smiled. 'Aha! So she *is* here!'

Eustace frowned. 'Not everything is as it seems. Not everything is black and white, especially not at the Embassy of Dead. Bad things are happening ... People are switching sides. But not Amber Chase – never.'

'Switching sides?'

'She's uncovered a plot. A plot that goes to the heart of the Embassy itself ... I've said too much already. You must leave this place immediately. It's not safe. They know she's on to them. They'll be coming to—'

He stopped suddenly as a scream pierced the quiet of the night.

The music from inside came to an abrupt halt, replaced by the sound of voices raised in panic. In the garden, everyone's eyes were trained on the sky as a dark shape, darker even than the night sky, loomed into view. It was peeling away from the blackness, as if it was formed from the night's own shadow, flickering like black lightening as it descended on the assembled ghosts.

As the garden broke into panic, Eustace took a sip of his ever-present cocktail, then, pushing Cora and Jake ahead of him, ran for the door.

'Hurry. I fear we may already be too late . . .'

SHADOWFOLK

ustace, Cora and Jake pushed their way back into the house through the panicking crowds. Shouts of alarm had spread through the house now and people were rushing for the front door. Jake turned round to see the large turbaned man pushing against the flow of ghostly bodies, running towards the garden. And that's when Jake saw it – a second shadowy form, coming from the opposite direction, pooling out of the shadows on the other side of the room. They were trapped.

Jake stood stunned, frozen in fear as the terrified crowds pushed past him in both directions, until he felt himself hoicked with the curve of Cora's hockey stick towards the stairs where Cora and Eustace were heading.

'We need to find Amber,' said Eustace.

'And Zorro!' said Cora. She started leaping up the stairs two at a time, followed by Jake, and Eustace.

'What *are* those creatures?' asked Jake breathlessly.

'Shadowfolk ...' said Eustace. 'Minor demons from the Afterworld. Someone at the Embassy has got themselves some new pets. They're hunters ... they've been after Amber for a few days now ... We have to warn her!'

The sound of a loud cry came from the other end of the corridor.

'Amber!' shouted Eustace, pushing past Cora, cocktail glass still in his hand, and tearing down the corridor.

As he threw open the door, Jake and Cora saw two figures facing one another. One was a young woman, a mop of curly hair poking out from underneath a leather flying cap. He recognised her face from the corkboard in the briefing room of the Embassy of the Dead.

It was the pilot: Amber Chase.

It was the other figure, if you could call it that, that caused Jake to freeze in fear.

The creature had no solid form, but rather – like the apparition in the garden – it seemed to be formed from shadows itself, rising out of the room's darkest corner. As Jake looked at the creature, its form flashed and flickered, one moment solid flesh, the next mere shadow, as insubstantial as a puff of smoke.

How can you fight something like that? thought Jake, and as he did, the beast turned to look at him, taking in the intruders in the doorway through black holes that seemed to serve as eyes. It lifted its head and sniffed the air.

That's when Amber Chase struck. Shifting her weight on to her left foot and springing into the air, she twisted her body, spinning and extending her leg sharply into a kick, her foot thundering into the creature's chest just in that second when it flickered into solidity. The force of the kick drove the beast upwards and out of the open window, smashing through the glass and shattering it all around them. For a second, a shadowy clawed hand scrabbled for

purchase on what was left of the window frame, before it slipped from sight.

Amber Chase turned to Eustace. 'Thanks for the help, Eustace,' she said flatly.

Eustace leant against the doorway, feigning exhaustion, and took a sip of his cocktail. 'What would you do without me?' Then he looked at her, and his face became serious. 'You're wounded?'

She raised a hand to her face. A trail of thin, grey liquid stretched from the wound to her hand. 'It took me by surprise.'

'Shadow venom,' said Eustace, ushering Jake and Cora into the room and closing the door behind them. 'We need to get you to the Embassy, or ...' His voice trailed off, the implication clear.

By now, Amber was in obvious pain, though she was doing her best to hide it. 'But the plague demon will cross if I cannot meet my contact in the Afterworld and stop it!'

Jake and Cora exchanged a look. 'What's a plague demon?' groaned Jake.

Whatever it was, it didn't sound good. Things had started to get serious. Very serious. As if being attacked by Shadowfolk in a club for stray ghosts wasn't serious enough already.

'I thought this was about smuggling jewels, not demons,' said Jake. 'Portentia said you were involved.'

Amber Chase looked angry. 'Portentia!' she spat. 'It was she who was involved, not me. It all started when we were assigned Clay. He'd been a stray for years before they at last processed him, and passed his file our way. It seemed an easy case ... It clearly wasn't the brother that had betrayed him. We just had to prove it to him. But she wouldn't do it. That's when I realised – Portentia was delaying his Undoing on purpose. Rather than helping him pass on, she was keeping him here on the Earthly Plane ...'

Cora gasped. 'I knew it!' She looked at Jake. 'I *knew* you hadn't done anything impressive when you Undid him.'

Jake ignored Cora's comment, and turned to Amber. 'But why?'

'Errol Clay was running a smuggling racket and Portentia wanted in – she let him get away with it in return for precious Afterworld artefacts ... You see, there is a way between the worlds, in this very club.'

'From here? How? Where?'

Suddenly, Amber fell to her knees. She groaned in pain.

Eustace took her hand. 'Don't talk so much, darling, save your strength.' He took a silk hanky from his breast pocket and dabbed at the gash on Amber's face.

'I have to pass on my information! Before it's too late,' she said through gritted teeth. 'The worlds of the Earthly Plane and the Afterworld are like continents separated by a sea – the sea of the Eternal Void,' she explained. 'But the Eternal Void is not static. Like a sea, it laps against the shores, and rises and falls, and occasionally, when the tides are favourable, the Void falls low enough in places for the two realms to meet ...' She paused and looked at Jake. 'Places like here. In this building is a crossing, one of Clay's smuggling routes. It's accessible from midnight and by sun-up is closed again. And the demon ... it crosses at dawn.'

Amber paused and took a shaky breath. She looked sick and pale, as though she'd been poisoned.

'So we wait here for it and get it when it lands!' said Cora, swinging her hockey stick.

Amber smiled sadly. 'By the time it's here, it'll be too late. Malthus must never leave the Afterworld.'

'Malthus? What's that?' asked Jake.

'*Who*, you mean . . . Malthus is a plague demon from the Outerlands of the Afterworld. One of the last remaining.'

'What would Portentia want with a plague demon?' asked Cora.

'Portentia has no knowledge of this particular order. She just wants the jewels. She's being used. It's someone else. Somebody at the Embassy . . .'

'How do you know?' asked Cora.

'Because I told my handler, and he . . . he never appeared at our rendezvous. He betrayed me, or else was intercepted. I don't know which.'

'What is a plague demon anyway, and why bring one here?' asked Jake.

'The Afterworld Authorities are already stretched to the limit, overseeing the passage of souls from the

Earthly Plane. It would only take some kind of incident that greatly increased the flow of spirits to throw the whole Afterworld into chaos.'

'And by something that suddenly increased the flow of spirits you mean ... something that killed hundreds of people?' asked Jake.

Amber shook her head. 'No. Not hundreds of people ...' She looked Jake in the eye. '*Millions.*'

Cora and Jake looked at each other. 'But ... but why? What does that achieve?'

'Chaos nurtures evil,' said Amber. She was struggling to get the words out now, her face contorting with pain as she spoke each one.

Eustace nodded. 'That vast a number of spirits all passing at once will bring chaos to the Afterworld. If the Afterworld descends into chaos, the forces of Fenris will rise up to bring their own kind of order. The Authorities and the Embassy could fall and usher in ...'

'The Age of Evil,' finished Jake, his heart sinking. An age where demons ruled over the lives of the living and the dead, and no laws would exist to keep those worlds apart.

'Which is why,' said Amber, 'I have to cross and get this message to my contact on the other side before it's too late.' She tried to get up, grimacing with the exertion.

Eustace started forward. 'Darling, you're not strong enough. I need to get you to the Embassy, get you medicine . . .'

Amber let out a growl. 'There's no time for that . . .'

'Then let me go,' said Eustace, taking a large swig of his cocktail with a slightly shaky hand. 'I'm sure I'll be fine.'

Amber looked at him and smiled sadly. 'Eustace, dear, I'm not sure that's the best use of your skills.'

Eustace nodded. 'I have to say I agree with you.'

'You should stay with Amber,' said Cora firmly. 'We'll go.' She looked at Jake, eyes questioning.

Jake sighed. But what else could he say? He nodded.

Eustace looked up at him sadly. 'I'm afraid it's not that simple. You can't go the Afterworld, Jake. Your body would die as soon it leaves the Earthly Plane. It's not like going to the Embassy.'

Cora slammed her hockey stick on the floor. 'Then I'll go alone!'

'No way,' said Jake. He looked at Eustace. 'I have an idea . . .'

INVASION OF THE BODYSHIFTER

E ustace swilled the never-ending cocktail
round his glass. Then he took a sip, and
swallowed. He looked at Jake.

'I suppose it might work.'

Cora swung her hockey stick in the air. She
seemed almost excited at the prospect, which Jake
couldn't help think was more than a little insane,
given what they were about to do. He almost
wished he hadn't said it now. But it was too late,
and now the idea was out there he couldn't take it
back.

The plan was that Jake would leave his body in
the care of Eustace the shapeshifter, as he had done
once before. It couldn't be more dangerous than
leaving it with Bad Penny, he reasoned. At least
Eustace did it for his actual job.

Amber was barely awake now. She'd been slipping in and out of consciousness for the last few minutes. It didn't look good, but at least this way Eustace could stay with her, and hopefully get her to safety.

'So where's the crossing anyway?' said Cora.

Before Amber could answer, they heard a noise coming from the corner of the room.

'Zorro! You're here!'

The little fox had appeared suddenly as if from nowhere and trotted over to Jake.

'Where have you . . .?' Jake frowned. Zorro's fur was damp.

'How can a ghost fox get wet?' He looked up at Cora, who shrugged.

'Where have you been, Zorro?' He scratched Zorro behind the ears, and noticed a trail of muddy fox prints leading from the slightly ajar door of a wardrobe built into the wall of the room.

Jake walked across the bedroom and threw the doors of the wardrobe wide open. Inside on the floor of the wardrobe was an old suitcase, and a few tatty clothes hung from a rail above. The wardrobe was huge. Jake groped around for the back of it, peering into the darkness. But it wasn't the small dusty space he was expecting.

Cora appeared at his shoulder. 'What's going on?'

'See for yourself,' said Jake.

It had no wall at the back. Instead ... it went down. Wooden steps, damp and rotten, leading down until they disappeared into darkness.

Cora looked down at the steps. Then she looked up at Jake. 'A passageway to another world hidden in a wardrobe?' She rolled her eyes. 'How clichéd.'

A quiet voice came from the other side of the room, little more than a whisper. 'Go ...' said Amber, wincing with pain. 'Go! Take the message to my contact ...'

'How will we find them?' asked Jake urgently.

'The jetty ... they'll know what to do.'

Jake smiled grimly and walked over to Eustace.

Eustace reached out his hand to touch Jake on the shoulder, as he had once before.

Jake took a step backwards and ... out of his body. It was pretty weird seeing it tottering there without him. His 'meat suit', as Eustace would call it, standing awkwardly in the middle of the room, supported only by Eustace's hand on its shoulder. Eustace then stepped forward and disappeared inside. Jake's body twitched slightly, then looked round and said in Jake's voice, 'Goodbye, you two. I'll see you soon.' He glanced down at Amber. 'We both will, I hope . . .'

Jake nodded, looking down at his transparent hands.

Cora looked across at him. 'You look weird as a ghost.'

'There was literally someone downstairs dressed as a swan. I think I could look weirder.'

'Is this really the time for a tiff?' asked Eustace.

Just then they heard the sound of clattering footsteps rushing up the stairs, and voices.

'The Embassy?' asked Amber.

Eustace raised an eyebrow. 'They're here quickly.'

Jake turned to go through the wardrobe. Then he looked back at Amber and Eustace-in-his-body. 'Just to check . . . Are you *sure* we shouldn't just tell them? Maybe they could get your message across?'

'No!' said Amber, with more force than she'd mustered for a while. 'We can't trust them. GO! Please, before they see you ...' she said, her eyes pleading.

'Right then,' said Cora. 'One small step for woman, one giant leap for womankind ...' And first Cora, then Jake, then Zorro, all hurled themselves into the wardrobe, Jake just managing to close the doors behind them as the door to the attic room was violently kicked open.

THE CAPTAIN TO THE RESCUE

'Wormling! What the devil are you doing here?'

They were about to descend the steps at the back of the wardrobe when Jake heard his name, and immediately recognised the voice. He pressed his eye to the crack between the two old wardrobe doors.

The Captain.

He was facing Eustace. He thought that Eustace was Jake. Well he was, kind of, but not really.

Jake's spirit blinked.

Why doesn't Eustace say something?

This changed everything, didn't it? The Captain was an ally, they could tell him what had happened and he could—

Jake was about to open the door when he felt Cora's hockey stick holding him back.

Wait! she mouthed.

There was someone else in the room too. A woman came into view.

Portentia!

She smoothed her dress. 'Hello, Wormling. Well, well, well . . . what are you doing mixed up with Amber Chase? Don't tell me you're a smuggler too?'

Eustace-in-Jake's-body stood up from the body.

'You know very well she's not a smuggler,' he said with barely contained rage. 'She doesn't have much time left. We need to get her back to the Embassy. She's been poisoned.'

'I'm not sure how much help we can give to traitors,' said the Captain, looking at Portentia.

Portentia seemed to be wavering. She whispered to the Captain, 'Yes, but we can't just leave them here to die, can we?'

'We're not traitors,' shouted Eustace. '*You're* the traitors. Some handler you are!' he said, looking at the Captain.

Cora and Jake shared a look. The Captain was Amber's handler? He couldn't be a traitor, could he?

'And what's more,' Eustace continued, 'I demand—'

'SILENCE!' shouted the Captain. 'I'm thinking.'

The Captain looked from Amber, to Eustace, to Portentia, a smile spreading across his face as a plan seemed to form in his mind.

'Take them to your place, Portentia. They'll be safe there,' he said, adding with a smile, 'for now. GUARDS!'

A moment later, two huge men entered the room. At the Captain's command, they grabbed Eustace-in-Jake's-body and bundled him from the room. 'Then come back for her,' added the Captain with a nod at Amber, who was by now lying unconscious on the floor.

Jake felt sick. Cora looked at him, clearly realising the same thing at the same time . . .

Amber's message hadn't been intercepted. The Captain had betrayed her. The Embassy's second-in-command was trying to bring a plague demon to the Earthly Plane that would lead to the death of millions of the living and allow the forces of Fenris to bring about an Age of Evil.

Unless they stopped it. Before the sun came up.

Jake was still reeling from the shock of this realisation, so much so that he nearly didn't notice when the Captain started making his way to the wardrobe.

'Quick!' hissed Cora, grabbing him and roughly pulling him down the stairs. They crouched there in the darkness, just out of view, as the doors swung open and the Captain grabbed the dusty old suitcase from the wardrobe floor, then slammed the doors shut again. As soon as he'd gone, Jake and Cora crept back up the stairs and watched again through the gap as the Captain dumped the suitcase on the edge of the bed and opened it.

'The latest shipment of illicit contraband has arrived.' He chuckled. 'I made a fortune in the war this way, don't you know? Back in my living days. No reason to stop making money just because you're dead.'

Portentia leant forward to look into

the suitcase.

'They're beautiful,' she breathed. She looked at the Captain. 'I never understood what you do with all the money, though.'

The Captain smiled. 'Oh, I'm not in it for the money,' he said, and reached into the suitcase. 'The wonder of the Afterworld is as boundless as the Eternal Void itself.' From inside the suitcase he took out a small box. He flicked it open and took out a ring. He held it up to the light, and it sparkled brightly.

'For you! Forged from a precious metal found only in the Afterworld,' he said, flicking it towards her. 'For all you've done.'

Portentia gasped with joy as she pushed it on her finger. 'It's beautiful.'

The Captain chuckled. 'A perfect fit. It's as though it were made for you!'

There was a groan from the floor. Amber Chase had rolled over. She was reaching out to the Captain.

The Captain smiled. 'She's strong . . .'

From the gap in the wardrobe doors, Jake could

see the form of Amber beginning to flicker back into life.

A flash of concern crossed Portentia's face. She looked at the Captain. 'She knows too much.'

'Don't worry,' said the Captain. 'She will be dealt with later.'

Amber groaned again. Like she was trying to say something. She grabbed at Portentia's foot. 'Malth ...' she managed with great effort, then again, 'Malthus ...'

Portentia looked at the Captain. 'What is she trying to say?'

The Captain frowned. 'Must be the poison. Fetch those guards, Portentia, and take the traitors to yours. I'll tidy things up with the Embassy and meet you there in the morning.'

'As you wish.' She turned and walked from the room.

The Captain watched Portentia leave, then knelt down by the fallen body of Amber Chase.

'You nearly told her, didn't you?' he said, placing a hand on her cheek. 'You nearly told her about the plague demon. The plague demon that will send her and millions of others to an early grave. The plague demon that will cause so much disruption that the forces of Fenris will be able to rise up, and win!' He smirked.

Amber Chase lifted her head from the floor. 'Why?' she croaked. 'You are a ghost!'

The Captain smiled. 'Those of us who change sides early enough will be rewarded.' He looked towards the door. 'Portentia knows nothing of the grand plan. How typical of a woman to think of only baubles and trinkets.'

Jake watched Cora's face redden with rage. He held a finger to his lips. To Jake's horror, his slight movement caused the door of the wardrobe to swing open a few inches. Jake held his breath until the Captain's back was turned, then he reached out and pulled it closed again.

The clicking sound of the door closing was almost inaudible. Almost. The Captain's head turned sharply. He was looking directly at the wardrobe.

Jake watched, frozen in fear, as the Captain started to move towards them. He felt a tug on his trousers. It was Cora. She was several steps down now, motioning him urgently to join her.

Without thinking of the consequences, Jake ran down the steps, and into another world.

PLAGUE DEMONS

OCCURRENCE:
Rare

DEMONIC TAXONOMY OF PLAGUE DEMONS:
Plague demons are a tiny subgroup of composite demon*, i.e. those demons whose physical form is made from a swarming of smaller micro-demons. Plague demons differ from usual composite demons in that the process of attracting and controlling micro-demons creates a pestilent residue†. This residue is of no effect to other celestial beings and of only minor effect to ghosts, however it can be harmful to the living should the demon arrive on the Earthly Plane (see later).

AFTERWORLD EXISTENCE:
Plague demons live as other demons within the Afterworld, usually in peace with the Afterworld Authorities.

---

* Akenbole, Wagstaff, Feg 2012, 'Composite Demons and their ilk'. *Journal of Demonology* p.1023

† Wong, Especius the Divine et al, 'Toxic Chemical Compounds of the Daemon Realm'. *Chemus Quarterly* p.234

PLAGUE DEMONS AND YOU:

Transference to the Earthly Plane seldom occurs as most micro-demons will not survive passage between the worlds unless the composite demon is safely bound within a vessel of some sort. On arrival in the Earthly Plane, a host must be found and inhabited, whereupon the micro-demons will be able to take a physical, earthly form. This gestation and hatching process usually takes around six hours. The process destroys firstly the host and secondly the plague demon itself, leaving the composite micro-demons to distribute across the Earthly Plane carrying with them the pestilent residue.

KNOWN CASE STUDIES:

Plague demons are rare in the Afterworld and little is known of each demon and its effect until they reach the Earthly Plane. The successful gestation and birthing of Esthus on the Earthly Plane, better known there as the Black Death, resulted in 25 million new spirits from across Europe passing to the Afterworld.

Not all plague demons carry human disease. The successful gestation and birth of Pensus led to outbreaks of guinea pig flu across South America. These are the only known cases of plague demons reaching the Earthly Plane, although several more plague occurrences are suspected of being originally demon-born.

THE PHONE CALL

Being in a living body had its advantages, but to be honest, to a man as vain as Eustace Carmichael-Bancombe, it would never live up to inhabiting his own body. Maybe that's why he'd ended up as a Bodyshifter – destined to spend his death-time learning the humility that came with inhabiting less-than-perfect people's bodies. He'd led a charmed life. He'd spent his early years enthusiastically getting himself expelled from a string of exclusive boarding schools. Unluckily for him, his father, an influential member of parliament, had pulled some strings and secured him a place at Oxford University, an establishment that hadn't suited him either. The Dean of his college spent the three years of his studentship trying to prevent him from being sent down – a fancy term for being expelled (again). Eventually he'd drifted into the shameful business of acting, where he'd managed to bag some minor roles in a number of bad plays. He might never have been as famous as he would've liked, but he was a big star in his own tiny galaxy until, one fateful evening, leaving his private members' club, cocktail glass still in hand, he paused midway through crossing the road to admire the reflection of himself and his new silk cravat in the window of a parked car.

'Why Eustace, you are a remarkably handsome—'

The unfinished sentence was destined to be his last. Eustace Carmichael-Bancombe was struck down by one of the first diesel-powered double decker buses, his beautiful body spread across Oxford Street. His last visual memory of life was the reflection of his face, contorted with pain.

Not a good look.

Eustace-in-Jake's-body had been held by the two Embassy guards as per the Captain's orders, while several other guards had cleared the Hangman's Club of Shadowfolk. Each was armed with a Demon Lance, a long stick with a small stone on the business end that could trap and contain a minor demon on contact.

Eustace-in-Jake's-body looked up as Portentia came down the stairs.

'The Captain wants you,' she said to the men who were guarding him. 'I'll take Wormling from here.'

Eustace recognised Portentia, of course. As the cloakroom attendant at the Embassy of the Dead, he'd even inhabited Portentia's body. Portentia had to follow the Embassy rules like any other member of the living: *leave your life at the door* and all that.

Portentia had not recognised Eustace, though. She only saw Jake's body. Eustace didn't take this personally – it was an occupational hazard.

He did, however, take it personally when she snarled, grabbed him roughly by the scruff of his neck and marched him over to her car, before opening the boot and, with another guard's assistance, bundling him inside and slamming it closed.

Eustace lay in the dark for a bit, trying to control Jake's body's breathing. He could feel himself panicking. He needed to keep Jake's body alive, both for Jake's sake and his own. He took a deep breath and held it. All was quiet.

A tiny voice spoke from somewhere within Jake's trousers: a woman's voice.

'Hello? Jake?'

He put Jake's hand in Jake's pocket and pulled out the offending piece of equipment the voice seemed to be coming from. One of those new portable telephones – a mobile! He looked at it suspiciously and tried to make the voice stop.

'Hello? Jake? It's Mum,' said the woman's voice again out of the loud speaker.

'I say,' spluttered Eustace in Jake's voice.

'Hello, love, are you there? You've called me. I'm at work. It's my night shift.'

'Hello?' said Eustace cautiously.

'Is everything OK, Jake? It's the middle of the night.'

Eustace thought for a second. *Is everything OK with Jake?* A quick summary of things to say flashed through his mind.

It's the most tiresome thing ... you see, Jake's body has been separated from his soul and has been locked in a car boot. Oh and a plague demon is due to arrive on earth in around six hours' time and wipe out most of the living population of earth. Probably including you and everyone you know.

He decided against. 'I just telephoned you by mistake, Mother. I'm awfully sorry. I must have rolled over on my telephone in my sleep.' He fake yawned. 'Anyway, back to beddy-byes!'

'Mother? Beddy-byes?' said Jake's mum. 'Just go back to sleep, love. I'll phone you in the morning.'

There was a pause. Then she added . . .

'I love you, Jake.'

Eustace blinked. His mother had never said such a thing. It felt nice. For the first time in almost 125 years of life and death, he was lost for words.

He should probably say something similar back.

'I-I'm awfully fond of you too, Mother,' he stuttered.

Jake's mum laughed. 'You silly sausage,' she said.

Eustace smiled. He liked Jake's mum.

Then the boot of the car opened again and Portentia reached in and snatched Jake's phone.

'I think I'll take that.'

She waved her hand in front of Jake's face and whispered some words.

Eustace felt Jake's body go limp and his eyes close. Like Jake's body had suddenly fallen asleep. Then the boot slammed shut again and everything went black.

THE OUTERLANDS

J ake and Cora stood in silence beneath the stars, water lapping at their feet.

The infinite blackness of the night sky was reflected in a calm sea that stretched into the distance before them until it was no longer clear where the sea ended and the night began. The mudflats they stood on seemed to extend endlessly too, to the left and the right and for miles behind, groupings of shifting islands of mud split by a myriad of small streams and rivulets all winding their way forwards, draining their black waters into the sea that Jake and Cora now faced, a sea as still as death itself.

Jake looked across at Cora, who – like she had been in the Embassy of the Dead – was now completely solid.

She looked at him looking at her. Then looked down at herself and shrugged, before turning her eyes back to the scene in front of them.

'If this is the Afterworld, then I hope I'm never Undone.'

Jake scratched his head and watched as Zorro hopped into a shallow rivulet that flowed between their island and a larger one that, as well as a few sproutings of seaweed and samphire, also sported a large wooden post. 'What are we supposed to do now?'

Zorro was struggling to get on to the next island. Jake tried to step across too, but slipped in the mud, one foot falling back into the flow, and immediately felt the source of Zorro's discomfort. The water was tugging at him with an almost irresistible force, pulling him downwards and towards the sea. He heaved his leg from the water and climbed on to the larger neighbouring island, then reached out for Zorro and pulled him up too. He held his hand for Cora, but she ignored it and took a running leap, clearing the river and landing on Jake and Zorro's island, the momentum nearly

– but not quite – carrying her off into the water on the other side.

Jake crouched down and cupped his hand in the water. Now he could see it close up, he realised it wasn't water at all. Instead it was as if he was holding a tiny spinning galaxy of night sky. He opened his fingers and watched the darkness drain through them, and as it fell, it was as though it was caught in an imperceptible breeze, carrying it like a cloud of smoke out towards the sea.

Except it wasn't the sea.

He looked out over the calm blackness that stretched before him, and remembered Amber's words at the club:

The worlds of the Earthly Plane and the Afterworld are like continents separated by a sea – the sea of the Eternal Void.

'I think this dark water is the Eternal Void.'

He'd seen the Void before. It seemed so long ago. A hole cut in the sky by the blade of a grim reaper's scythe. He shuddered at the memory of being pulled closer and closer to oblivion.

'I am not going anywhere near that water again,' he said.

'And if that small stream can cause Zorro problems, think how a dip in the sea would feel.'

Jake nodded grimly. 'So what do we do? We're stuck on the edges of nowhere, no one knows we're here and the entire population of the living world is about to be wiped out by a demonic plague.'

He sighed and leant against the tall ancient-looking post that projected from the marshy ground. It was wet from the mist.

'And now my hoodie's soaking wet.'

Cora began pacing the island. 'All we have to do is find the jetty. If we can alert Amber's contact, we could stop all this!' She punched the air. 'Cora Sanderford saves the world!' She paused and looked at Jake. 'Again!'

Jake decided to ignore the fact that he had been partly responsible for saving the world last time too. 'So how do we get there?' He looked across the mud flats. The mist was rolling in fast and they could barely see twenty metres. 'And where is "there" anyway?'

He ran his fingers through his hair. It seemed hopeless.

Cora, on the other hand, was smiling. 'I'm not sure what will happen, but whatever does, it probably happens by one of us ringing that.'

She pointed her hockey stick into the air above Jake's head.

He turned to look at where she was pointing. Another smaller piece of wood was nailed to the top of the post he'd been leaning against. A small bell was hanging from it, suspended by a short length of rope.

Jake looked at Cora.

'I guess we've got nothing to lose,' he sighed. He reached up and grabbed a scrap of old cloth that hung from the bell's clapper and yanked.

The bell made a short dull *clank*. Deadened by the mist, it seemed strangely underwhelming. He looked at Cora.

'Well . . . That was a bit of an anti-climax.'

Then, from nearby – its source hidden in the rolling mists – a different bell answered its chime.

THE BOATMAN

The ringing grew louder as through the mists a small wooden boat appeared. A man stood at the back, pushing into the black waters with an oar to propel the craft through the narrow channels and out of the mist.

'Oh, look! It's just like the punts we used to use when we visited St Swithins' School for Boys!' said Cora, clapping her hands in delight.

'I hope not. We'll need more than a punt to get us across the Eternal Void.'

Cora waved excitedly at the man as he approached. He was a grizzled, barrel-chested figure, with a white beard, and woolly hat. An oilskin coat was wrapped tightly around him.

As the craft bumped against the shore, Jake could see a strange creature tethered to the boat's prow. It was a small furry thing, with a fluffy, round body the size of a grapefruit, large trusting eyes, and a thin beak, like a pencil.

'Oh. My. Goodness!' spluttered Cora. 'It so cute! What's its name?'

The man stepped from the craft with a rope and wrapped it around the pole. Then he took a paper bag from his pocket and pulled out a long worm and passed it to Jake.

'It doesn't have a name. It's a Foreboder. It needs feeding if you want passage. And keep that fox away from it.'

Jake held the worm blankly, unable to stop looking at a tattoo of a strange and evil-looking bird-like creature that was inked on the man's powerful forearm.

'The Foreboder,' the man said. 'Feed it the worm.' He took a pipe from his pocket and started stuffing it with tobacco.

'Right,' said Jake. He held up the earthworm for the tethered creature, who blinked at him, then gently plucked it from his grasp and gulped it down with a sudden jerk of its neck.

'Who are you anyway?' the boatman barked.

Cora narrowed her eyes. 'Who are *you*?'

The man looked at her. 'None of your business,' he said. He put the pipe in his mouth and struck a match against the boat, lighting the tobacco. It stank.

Cora pulled a disapproving face.

The boatman looked around. 'You with ... Clay?' he muttered, the pipe clenched between his yellowed teeth.

'Of course we are,' said Cora confidently.

'So did they get the suitcase? I left it at the top of the stairs just like Mr Clay likes.'

Jake thought back to the suitcase of jewellery that the Captain had opened. 'Yes. They got it.'

The man rubbed his hands together. 'I'm supposed to be doing one more run and then Mr Clay will let me back into the Earthly Plane.'

He blew out a cloud of rank smoke.

Jake didn't like to tell him that Errol Clay no longer lived on the Earthly Plane.

The man coughed again. 'And not before time. This swamp is making me sick. So much for the

Afterworld being free of mortal illness.' He paused.

'Why you here anyway? The next delivery's not till dawn.'

Jake and Cora exchanged an excited look. This was just the confirmation they needed!

'Erm . . . Mr Clay wants us to deliver a message,' lied Jake. 'There's someone waiting for us . . . A spirit from the Afterworld. Can you take us?'

'Well, where do you want to go?'

Jake looked at Cora. 'To the jetty,' she said calmly.

As Jake looked at the man and waited for his response, for the first time he saw his face clearly. It was deathly pale and clammy, with tired, sunken eyes.

He wiped sweat from his brow. 'You want me to take you across the Void, do you?' He thought for a moment, then shrugged. 'If Clay wants me to smuggle people to the Afterworld instead of jewels to the Earthly Plane, that's his business. I can get you to the old jetty.' He coughed and spat into the Void-waters. 'Did you bring a sacrifice?' he asked suddenly.

'I'm sorry? A what?' said Jake.

The man looked over Jake's head, peering into the mist, his eyes settling on Zorro. 'It doesn't matter. Everyone in! Next stop . . . the Afterworld.'

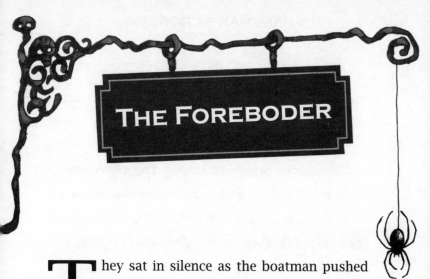

THE FOREBODER

They sat in silence as the boatman pushed the craft off the mudflats and out into the deeper waters of the Void. Once he could no longer touch the bottom, he sat back down, taking up both oars and settling into a steady rhythm.

As the water got deeper, so the mist became thicker. Jake looked back over his shoulder. The banks they'd left a moment ago could barely be seen now, just a tiny sliver of grey cutting the black of the sky and the Void-waters in two. Up ahead the mass of Void – the silent sea – waited, dark and infinite.

In the distance, rising from the waters, a shape loomed – what looked to be a huge concrete pillar, its top lost within the mist. Further along, another could be seen, and then, as they drifted forwards, another.

'What are they?' asked Jake.

'That's the bridge, of course. From one side to the other. Some go under, but those with sense go over.' He dipped his pipe into the Void, extinguishing the flame. 'Lest they see the glow. Won't be doing to take chances.' He shook his head. 'As we speak, the souls of today's new dead – those that pass easy – be traipsing across that very structure on their way to Deadhaven, City of the Dead.'

'Sounds like a cheery place,' muttered Cora.

He shrugged. 'I wish *I* were there. Beats rowing this old crate across the Void-waters for months on end, waiting for Clay to let me back into the Earthly Plane.'

Jake looked at him and frowned. A small trickle of red was dripping from the man's nose. A vivid stain on his snow-white beard. 'Your nose is bleeding.'

The boatman scowled and wiped the blood away. He began to say something, but stopped abruptly as the Foreboder let out a quiet mewing sound.

A moment later, Zorro let out a growl too.

Jake looked over at him. His ears were pricked up. 'What is it, boy?' said Jake, stroking his furry companion.

The boatman looked around the river, nervously. 'We can't be . . .' he whispered. 'Unless . . .'

'Unless what?' asked Jake, sharing a look with Cora.

'Curse this fog!' muttered the boatman. The Foreboder's whimpering grew louder and it was hopping nervously at the end of its leash. Jake reached out to pet the strange creature.

The boatman stopped him. 'Stay completely still,' he hissed. 'The Foreboder is serving its purpose. It warns us of danger.'

And still they stayed, all listening intently, though neither Jake nor Cora knew what they were listening for. The boat drifted silently on the water, pulled along by the tide, until there was a dull *thunk* as the boat struck something.

'Dry land?' asked Cora, turning to the boatman with a note of hopefulness in her voice.

But the boatman didn't reply. He was looking over the edge of the boat at the source of the bump

– a branch, poking from the water, thick and wet and dark with algae. It was as though a giant tree was growing beneath the tides, the very top of its crown emerging from the waters. Leafless. Dead.

'The Hangman's tree,' whispered the boatman, a look of dread upon his face. 'We'll be well served to make haste from this doomed location.'

The boatman grabbed his oars and started rowing frantically away from the tree, but the tide was strong and kept pulling him back. Suddenly the boat lurched, as if caught on a rolling wave. Jake fell forwards, breaking his fall by grabbing the bow of the boat.

By his hand was the Foreboder's leash ... but nothing was tethered to its end.

'The Foreboder ...' shouted Jake to the boatman. 'It's gone!' But the words died in his throat as his gaze followed Cora's. She was staring at the water a few metres from the boat with a look of horror on her face as, from the depths of the Void, something rose up ... then slowly sank back into the water.

'It's the Hangman!' hissed the boatman,

moaning in terror.

'The H-Hangman?' stuttered Jake. 'What's that?'

The boatman sprang into action, rowing away from the tree with renewed vigour.

'The Hangman is the Void-demon that guards these waters. Why do you think it's called the Hangman's Crossing? It plucks its prey from the surface and hangs them in the branches of its tree.'

Cora's grip tightened on her hockey stick. 'Its prey?'

The boatman looked at her. 'Us.'

Jake peered out into the mist. Once again the Void-waters were as dark and still as the night sky. 'Has it gone?'

As if to answer his hopeful question, the boat lurched forwards again, as though a gigantic creature had swum beneath them.

The boatman moaned in terror, and shook his head. 'It's waiting. The flesh of the Foreboder will not be enough to satisfy its appetite. We can't get away. It's useless,' he said, putting the oars down. 'We must ready the sacrifice. The Hangman must be fed.'

Jake and Cora looked at each other. 'What

sacrifice?' Jake asked.

'The fox, you fool. Throw it the fox!'

Jake stood up and the boat rocked. 'No!'

The boatman stood too, an ugly look on his face. He tried to push past Jake, reaching out for Zorro, who snarled.

'I won't let you,' said Jake, standing his ground. Now Cora tried to stand too and the boat rocked dangerously from side to side. She stumbled and fell into the hull.

The boatman grabbed Jake by his hoodie. '*You'll* have to do then,' he said, an evil smile on his face.

But Jake wasn't looking at the boatman. He was looking past him at what was rising from the deep.

No more than ten metres from them, a giant bird-like head rose from the water, followed by a vast, feathered body, glistening with the moisture of the Void. It was towering above them, three times bigger than the boat at least. As its coal-black eyes settled on them, it spread its giant wings, opened its savage beak and released a shriek that ripped through the silence, and shook the boat.

'Watch out!' cried Jake, as the Hangman struck.

But it was too late. The beast's giant beak descended on the turning boatman, grabbing him by the torso and beginning to lift him from the boat. Jake grabbed on to the boatman's arms, desperately trying to keep the terrified man in the boat, trying to save him from his fate, but the pull of the Hangman became too strong and Jake lost his grip, tumbling back into the bottom of the boat.

He watched, frozen in terror, as the boatman was held above the waters for a second – just long enough for Jake to take in the expression of horror on his face – before the creature took him beneath the surface, disappearing beneath the dark surface of the waters with a quiet splash, his screams extinguished by the Void.

All was still.

Jake looked at Cora. They were lying in an awkward heap in the hull of the gently rocking boat, too frightened to move.

'Do you think it's gone?' he whispered. He stood tentatively and looked over the side of the boat in the direction of where the boatman had disappeared, and as he did so the boat lurched violently one more time. His fingers clawed at the side of the craft, but it was too late. With barely enough time to take a breath he tumbled over the side and into the Eternal Void.

Into the Hollow of the Hangman's Tree

It took Jake a moment to realise that he could breathe beneath the surface of the Void. But the momentary relief this knowledge gave him was soon replaced by a growing sense of dread. He was sinking. Sinking into the black depths of the Void. Deeper and deeper.

The phosphorescent glow of tiny creatures, bundled into tiny galaxies, small enough to fit in his hand, lit the darkness – it would've been beautiful, if it hadn't been for the fact that he was in the Eternal Void.

Something scratched against his face and snagged on his clothes, his downward journey suddenly halted by the branches of the Hangman's tree.

And that's when Jake saw them – skeletons, draped in the limbs of the tree, lit by softly glowing creatures that darted amongst the bones and leafless branches.

There were the bones of many Foreboder-like creatures, and others – strange remains Jake didn't recognise. But there were human skeletons too ... Jake wondered if they were all like the boatman and himself, ghosts (temporary or otherwise) that shouldn't have ever set foot in the Afterworld.

There was the sound of cracking twigs and Jake looked down to see the creature known as The Hangman pulling itself around the branches in the darkness below, its claws nimbly gripping the branches as it threaded its way around its lair. There was no sign of the Boatman – Jake tried not to think about the man's fate. A fate he might end up sharing if he didn't get away. Jake started to pull himself upwards, his hands gripping around the slimy, black branches of the tree.

Higher and higher he climbed, twisting to the other side of the tree, putting the trunk between himself and the Hangman until finally the Hangman disappeared behind him, hidden in the murky depths. Jake stopped for breath, pausing for a moment on a thick branch that grew from beneath a rotten hollow.

There was a loud echoing crack as the branch snapped and drifted away into the Void. Jake froze in terror as the Hangman's head suddenly appeared from the deep, its bird-like eyes boring upwards, probing the darkness for its prey. Jake jerked his head away, out of the Hangman's line of vision, but he could hear the beast coming his way, dragging itself around the tree. Jake looked around in a panic, desperately searching for somewhere he could hide himself. His eyes settled on the rotten hollow in the tree. He took a deep breath and squeezed himself into the cavity. Just in time – the beast's giant bird head appeared, inspected the cracked branch and, finding nothing, retreated.

In the pitch black of the hollow, Jake caught his breath, waiting till he was absolutely sure the bird-beast was gone. Then, slowly, he pushed himself out of the hole. As he did so, he realised something had caught on his sleeve and was pulling him back. He turned to see what it was.

It was the cord of a necklace, and at its end was a bright white pendant, swinging back and forth with the sway of the water. Jake reached out his hand to touch it as if compelled, wondering at its smoothness, and also – feeling its tip – its sharpness. And just like that the necklace broke off in his hand, as though it had been rotting away for years just waiting for someone to claim it, and now it was his.

As his fingers closed around it, Jake experienced a sudden flash of light and a violent gust of wind, whooshing all around him like a spinning vortex. Or at least he thought he did, because a second later – it was gone. Jake paused – had the Hangman felt it? Would it come for him again? He peered out from the hole in the tree trunk, waiting to see if the Hangman would emerge. But it was nowhere to be seen.

Jake placed the broken necklace and its strange pendant in his pocket and began once more to climb upwards, pulling himself from bough to bough, fighting, always fighting, against the pull of the Eternal Void. It felt as though for every step nearer to the surface he took, an invisible force increased, trying to pull him back down again, until he felt he couldn't go on. He was so tired that he just couldn't hold on any more and his grip on the tree weakened and he felt himself letting go . . . Now he was drifting from the tree, drifting once more in the darkness of the Void, amongst the swirling galaxies and constellations of lights, the tiny glowing creatures of the Void-waters . . . *Or are they stars in the sky?* Jake thought as at last he gave up and lost consciousness.

Jake woke to a familiar wet licking feeling on the side of his face.

'Zorro?' He opened his eyes. It *was* Zorro, and above him – a starry sky.

He had made it!

Zorro nuzzled him, burying his muzzle into Jake's neck.

He pushed himself up and looked around. He was sitting on a small pebbly beach that rose in a gentle curve up from the Void-waters below.

'Jake!' shouted Cora as she ran towards him, nearly knocking him over again as she wrapped her arms around him. 'I thought you would never wake up!'

'I'm quite surprised I have!' he said. 'What happened?'

Cora let go of him. She was trying her best to be cross.

'I don't know but you're an idiot trying to save the boatman. He was going to murder Zorro!' She crouched down and held Zorro's head between her hands, gazing into the fox's eyes. 'You poor little thing.'

'Poor Zorro?!' said Jake. 'What about me? I'm the one who just took a dip in the Eternal Void and narrowly escaped being eaten alive by the world's scariest vulture thing.'

'Well exactly. You're an idiot. Don't scare me like that again,' said Cora. 'You're supposed to be the living one. The dynamic of our relationship doesn't work if you're not boringly normal.'

'How long was I under the water for?' said Jake, scratching his head.

200

'No idea,' she replied. 'We found you washed up on the beach when we got here. Think you must've passed out from shock. You know that's not the best trait for somebody who's co-responsible for the fate of the entire living world.'

She looked away. 'It's good to have you back, though.'

There was an awkward silence, then Cora executed a downwards smash with her hockey stick, no doubt splitting the head of an imaginary foe, thought Jake with a fond smile.

'It felt like I was gone for ages . . .' Jake paused. 'Oh yes, and I saw something . . .' he said as a memory floated back to him. His fingers reached for his pocket, but the necklace wasn't there. He felt a stab of sharp disappointment, then instinctively reached for his neck. Through the fabric of his hoodie he could feel something – it was the pendant! He could feel the length and sharpness of it. It seemed the cord was now tied safely around his neck. He couldn't remember fastening it, but he supposed he must have done. He tugged it out from under his hoodie so he could inspect it more closely.

'What's that?' asked Cora, leaning closer.

Jake ran his hand through his hair. 'I don't know ... I ... I found it.'

Cora looked at it. 'It looks like a tooth,' she said, inspecting it, but before Jake could reply, the sound of feet crunching on pebbles made them both turn.

A tall thin figure was walking down the beach towards them, face partly hidden in the shadow of a top hat.

'Well, it most certainly weren't you two that I was expecting to find at the meeting place,' said the figure.

A huge smile spread across Jake's face and he started to run towards the old man.

'Stiffkey!'

Stiffkey removed his top hat and opened his arms for Jake to run into.

'It's good to see you, boy!' A smile cracked his solemn face. 'Even if you do appear to be dead!' He gave Jake a big hug, then put his hands on Jake's shoulders and looked at him.

'Don't worry,' said Jake, 'it's only temporary. I hope! You remember Cora?'

'Aye,' said Stiffkey, giving the ghostly schoolgirl a nod and a smile. 'She's not someone you forget in a hurry!'

'How's the Afterworld treating you?' asked Cora.

On their first meeting, Jake remembered Stiffkey resembling a sombre-looking wading bird. All thin legs and long nose. Now, he still looked like a bird, but this time one in full flight. His stoop was still visible but now it was less apologetic and more purposeful, his black coat catching in the wind like the wings of a raven. Jake smiled up at the old ghost. He still had a deathly grey face, but maybe he'd looked that way alive.

Stiffkey smiled at Cora. 'Can't complain. So you two gonna tell me what you be doing here on this godforsaken jetty? You've got a message for me to pass on to the Authorities?'

Jake sighed with relief. Suddenly he realised how tired he was, and how grateful to be with someone who would know what to do.

Slowly, between him and Cora, they managed to piece together everything that had happened – from Jake Undoing Clay, to his weird confession, to finding Eustace and Amber at the Hangman's Club, the Shadowfolk, and worst of all – the Captain revealing himself to be a traitor, and his horrible plan.

The old undertaker pulled his hands down his sagging face.

'So, boy, let's be clear, for these be serious allegations you be flinging around. You say the

Captain – he who works at the Embassy – is plotting for a plague demon to arrive on the Earthly Plane. And that that demon is on its way as we speak?'

Jake nodded. 'Amber overheard the plans. It will arrive at dawn, on the last shipment through the Hangman's Crossing.'

'Well, it can't go that way no more, not now the boatman's been lost. It'll have to go via the bridge. That's the only other one open at that time,' he said, replacing his hat thoughtfully. Then, after a moment, he reached into the folds of his long jacket and pulled out a small drab-coloured bird. Cradling it gently, he held it up to his mouth and whispered. A long sentence, it seemed. Then he gently threw the bird into the air, whereupon – to Jake and Cora's amazement – it disappeared!

'What was that?' asked Jake.

'Oh, just sending on a message ahead. Come, lad. We must get to that bridge.'

Jake nodded as he and Cora followed Stiffkey up the pebbly slope away from the Void-waters.

'I suppose he won't be hard to spot at least . . . The demon, I mean?'

'That ain't how it works, Jake,' explained Stiffkey. 'A demon doesn't just walk across the bridge, or even sneak through a portal. Few demons *want* to be on the Earthly Plane, nor would anyone allow them across willingly. It'll need to be trapped in something with Old Magic. An artefact of sorts. That's why the Authorities will have to scan everything and everyone trying to cross, and they may decide just to shut the bridge entirely. That'll be their choice. We just need to get there and tell them before that sun comes up,' explained Stiffkey, as the pebbled slope joined the edge of a thick forest. 'And if that demon's crossing at first light, we'll be wanting to get there pretty fast.'

THE CITY OF THE DEAD

The path through the forest obviously hadn't been used for some time. Jake, Cora and Stiffkey found themselves running to keep up with Zorro, who was clearly having the time of his death. It seemed like the wood was a second home to him, and he was certainly enjoying his new-found solidity. They watched as the fox weaved his way between ferns and beneath fallen, mossy branches, pausing to root around in the soft soil, and wee joyously up against a tree.

The dew hung heavy in the cold night air, another signal of the coming dawn, and it clung to their clothes, making Jake's jeans feel damp and heavy. The air felt clean here, though, and fresh, and as they ran along the path to their destination, Jake felt more alive than he had for ages.

Which was ironic. Because, technically, he was dead.

Looking up at the forest canopy that stretched above their heads, it was clear the sky was lightening. The stars had lost some of their brightness as night and day prepared to swap shifts.

It was beautiful ... but the strange dusky light meant something other than just the start of a new day in the Afterworld.

It meant they were running out of time.

They all realised it together and as one they increased their pace, relieved at least that this bit of the journey was downhill.

Soon the ground began to level out and in the murky distance ahead, the lights of a city could be seen.

'What's that place?' breathed Cora.

'That be Deadhaven,' said Stiffkey. 'The City of the Dead. Strange to think that most of those dead that be sleeping safe in their beds there now, have no knowledge of the machinations that are occurring to keep them safe ... They be like worms that know nothing of crows, till they poke their head above the freshly dug soil, of course. Likewise, those living on the Earthly Plane. They have no knowledge that the fate of their happy-ever-after lies in the balance.'

Jake looked at the twinkling lights of the City of the Dead and found himself thinking of his mum and dad. And Sab and Sammy. Were they all asleep now? Did they know he was missing? He hoped not. He hoped they never had to find out.

'And you, girl? The longings to pass kicked in yet?' Stiffkey raised an eyebrow at Cora. 'That city up ahead there is where you belong, after all. Ain't you sick of the living by now?'

Cora pulled a face. 'No one tells a Sanderford what to do. Anyway, seems to me I'm needed sorting out this mess on the Earthly Plane.'

Stiffkey laughed. 'You two ain't changed, I'm proud to say.'

'Commander, sir!'

Jake turned to see two masked men in military uniforms marching towards them. They had clearly been waiting to greet them.

Their leader ran up to Stiffkey and saluted. 'We got your message, Commander,' he said, the little bird appearing from nowhere and flying back into Stiffkey's pocket as he said it. 'Where do you need to go?'

Stiffkey turned to the soldier and nodded. 'To the bridge,' he said. 'And don't take your time about it.'

As they followed the men, Jake turned to Stiffkey. 'Commander?' he whispered with a raised eyebrow.

Stiffkey turned to Jake and winked. 'Seems like humble old Stiffkey got a promotion after he passed. In recognition of my long years of service to the Embassy.'

'Even for a dead undertaker,' said Jake, 'you really are a dark horse.'

THE BRIDGE

I t didn't take long to get to the bridge. The men had led them to a path that wound through scrubland and eventually on to a dirt track where an open-backed army lorry was parked.

A moment later, Cora, Jake and Zorro were being rattled around the back of the truck as it sped down the track towards the entrance to the bridge. Here and there were wooden shacks, temporary dwellings for the dead pausing on the long march to Deadhaven.

Soon the dirt track joined a wider road. Stiffkey took his pocket watch from his pocket and tapped it. 'We're almost there.'

Jake and Cora gawped as they took in an endless procession of people, trudging along the road in the opposite direction to them.

'Where are they going?' asked Jake.

'The recently passed,' explained Stiffkey. 'Making their way from the bridge to Deadhaven.'

There were so many of them.

'It's hard to believe so many people die each day,' said Jake. He tried not to think about what the crowd would look like if Malthus made it over the crossing.

Stiffkey nodded. 'Aye, and more coming with each passing day. It's as much as we can do to keep them safe. But there's plenty of space once they be here.'

Jake couldn't tear his eyes from the never-ending stream of people. Each one leaving behind best friends, a family, and a life, in the Earthly Plane.

'And what goes the other way?'

Stiffkey scratched his head. 'Mostly only officials from the Afterworld Authorities or the Embassy, spirits on special business in the Earthly Plane, occasionally a celestial creature like a reaper. Hence why there are so few checks in place – only the most trusted cross here.'

Jake chewed on his hoodie cord, thoughtfully. 'And once the checks *are* in place . . .?'

'A demon, even confined in an object, will radiate a detectable aura. Once they're looking for it, it should be easy to find. And no one crossing need know they're looking neither, so they won't be warned off to try again another time. We'll get 'em, Jake, don't worry.'

The lorry went over a bump and then the road became suddenly smooth as they hit the bridge.

'Look!' breathed Cora.

Ahead of them and on either side was the Void, its black waters disappearing into the mist. The bridge rose up out of mist, the massive concrete supports that Jake and Cora had seen from the boat looking like the legs of some gigantic beast wading through the sea, its long neck stooping and stretching towards the shore on the other side.

Ahead a barrier blocked their path.

'Will they let us straight across?' asked Cora. 'Or will they need to check Zorro for ghost-rabies or something?'

Stiffkey shook his head. 'Ghosts can't pass illnesses to other ghosts, or the living. Only thing makes you sick in the Afterworld is a plague demon, and even then, a ghost will only get slightly ill from such a creature. Nothing in comparison to what such demons do to the living.' He looked across the Void-waters. 'Last time such a demon got across they called it the Black Death, and it lead to twenty-five million new spirits crossing over at once. Almost broke the Afterworld that time too, and there weren't no traitors around then to take advantage. It will be a different story this time, make no mistake.'

Jake found his eyes drawn instinctively to the sky. Above the Void in the east, the sky was definitely lightening now. There were no stars, no moon, and a distinct pinky light was beginning to show along the horizon.

The lorry slowed to a stop and Stiffkey hopped from the back.

'We're at the checkpoint now, boy,' said Stiffkey with a glance across at Jake. 'Assuming these traitors are good timekeepers, we should be just on time.'

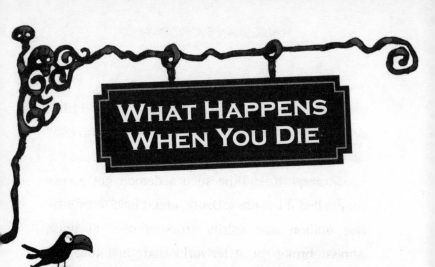

WHAT HAPPENS WHEN YOU DIE

Stiffkey, followed by Cora and Jake and Zorro, all ran as fast as they could towards the checkpoint.

The Afterworld seemed to have given Stiffkey a new lease of life – or rather a new lease of death. His long strides quickly took him to the front of the group, his black coat streaming behind him. There was no sign of the tired old undertaker he'd been on the Earthly Plane.

A guard stepped from the gloom, a torch in her hand.

'Commander! What gives us the pleasure?'

Jake and Cora squinted as the guard directed the beam of the torch into their faces.

She looked at Stiffkey. 'Commander?'

Stiffkey motioned for Jake and Cora to stay

where they were, while he went inside to talk to the guard. A few minutes later, the guard came out again.

'Sanderford and Green?'

Jake and Cora nodded and the guard indicated they should come inside too, handing over some paperwork to them as she did so. 'These papers will allow you to cross back to the Earthly Plane.' She frowned at Jake as she held the door for them to pass. 'You know, you are one of only a few living persons who have ever crossed to the Afterworld and returned.'

Cora looked at Jake. 'Finally you've done something of note!' she joked.

The guard didn't smile as she entered behind them and closed the door. Instead she looked at Stiffkey.

'We've put the added security in place now, as ordered. And you'll be relieved to know nothing has crossed to the Earthly Plane all night. If anything tries to cross now, we'll catch it, make no mistake. You'll understand, Commander, that given the threat, we'll have to scan you all for the presence of any hidden demons or contraband, just to be safe. Something could have been planted on any of you without you even knowing.'

Stiffkey nodded. 'Of course.'

The guard took a glowing stick from her pocket and proceeded to move it around Stiffkey's body. 'Now you,' she said, pointing to Cora.

Zorro was weaving around her ankles and so received his scan at the same time.

'All clear,' noted the guard. 'Now you ...' said the guard, coming towards Jake with her stick.

That's when Jake remembered the tooth. A sudden panic struck him. Was this contraband? Would he spend the rest of his life – or death – in an Afterworld prison? The guard started to wave her stick.

'Wait ...' he began, as the stick passed over the tooth beneath Jake's hoodie.

But the stick didn't register anything. The guard looked at him questioningly. 'Everything OK? You're clear to go through.'

Jake breathed a huge sigh of relief as he touched the tooth through his hoodie, checking it was still there. He was pleased he didn't have to part with it. How many other people could say they'd brought back a souvenir from the Afterworld?

'I er . . . yes, thanks,' he said.

'Well I think that's that then,' said the guard with a smile. 'Anything tries to cross, we'll be sure to keep it here till you get back,' she said to Stiffkey, with a respectful nod before waving them all on across the bridge.

They continued walking in silence a while. It was an eerie place, what with the Eternal Void beneath them, and the constant flow of the dead walking in the other direction.

'So that's that?' asked Jake.

'Seems so,' said Stiffkey.

'We did it?' asked Jake.

'Aye, lad, we did it,' Stiffkey replied as he stopped walking. 'And here we are.'

Ahead of them the bridge ended suddenly, as though they had stopped building it halfway across. Before them spanned an expanse of blackness that seemed to continue for ever. The other side of the bridge, if indeed there was one, was completely invisible.

Cora and Jake turned to Stiffkey, who placed a hand on each of their shoulders. 'There be a lot you two don't understand yet. And much of it you never will. I've been dead longer than you've been alive and it ain't all clear to me, and anyway now's not the time to explain ...'

Jake blinked. As they were standing there a figure had appeared from the air in front of them, landing at their end of the bridge – an old man. It was as though he'd stepped from thin air. The old man looked at them and smiled, and continued on his way past them, walking along the bridge to join the line of souls walking their way towards Deadhaven.

'Two humans die each second, they reckon,' said Stiffkey. 'And that's in a good second too. Sometimes it's more. Sometimes less. But the Earthly Plane never goes much more than that without someone leaving its soil.' He took his top hat off and held it in front of his body.

'They all end up on the end of this bridge, though, via the Embassy of the Dead.'

Cora stepped up to the end of the bridge and peered over the edge. The wind whipped around them, for they were many hundreds of metres above the Void-waters. She had to keep one hand on her straw boater to stop it blowing from her head.

'So we just step off the end of the bridge and we'll find ourselves at the Embassy?' she asked, shouting over the wind.

Stiffkey smiled. 'Try it if you like, but you'd just be plunging into the Eternal Void, girl. So I'd take a step back if I was you.' He reached into his coat and took out a clear plastic bag full of labelled black doorknobs. He took out one and inspected the label.

The Captain's Office. Embassy of the Dead.

'Those of us in the know have a shortcut. Old Magic. It's banned on the Earthly Plane but can be useful here.'

He held the doorknob over the end of the bridge, twisted it in the air, and pulled. Jake and

Cora gasped as, from nowhere, a door appeared and swung open.

Cora readied her hockey stick for battle with the Captain.

Stiffkey shook his head. 'This ain't no place for children,' he said. He took a different doorknob from his bag and tossed it to Cora and Jake. 'I'll handle things from here,' he said, before stepping into the darkness of the doorway and closing it behind him.

Cora looked at the doorknob, and sighed. *'Visitor's Waiting Room. Embassy of the Dead.'*

They'd been there before, of course. They would be processed by Hermann Poltago, the Summoner, thought Jake, and no doubt sent back to the Earthly Plane, perhaps with some minor Undoing assignment, if they were lucky that is, and they weren't banned from the Embassy for ever for disobeying rules.

'Boring!' muttered Cora and, for once, Jake found himself agreeing. It would be an anti-climax after saving the world, that's for sure, but still, it would be nice to see his mum and dad, and Sab.

Cora held the doorknob aloft over the edge of the bridge. With a sigh, she turned it in the air, pulling open a doorway, just as Stiffkey had done. Then she stepped through.

Now Jake was alone on the end of the bridge with Zorro. And he suddenly realised – this was where Zorro belonged, not with him back on the Earthly Plane.

He thought of how Zorro had been here in the Afterworld. Alive. Free. Solid. Finally able to do the things that foxes liked to do. Surely if any ghost deserved to be here in the Afterworld, it was him.

He crouched down to the little fox, who was looking up at Jake expectantly. Jake stroked his head and looked into his eyes.

Zorro tilted his head to one side questioningly. He could tell something was up. Jake felt a tear welling in his eye. He crouched there for a minute longer, holding the fox's head in his hands, all the time with Zorro looking back at him.

'You stay here, boy. There's a good fox. Goodbye, Zorro.'

Zorro lifted a back leg, licked his bum, then, ignoring his master completely, trotted on through the open doorway.

Jake smiled and, with a shrug, stepped through the door after him.

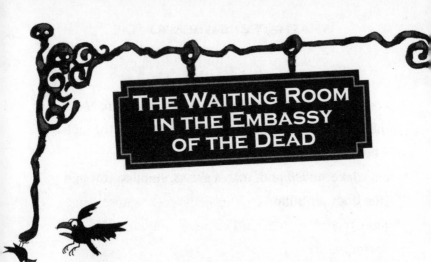

THE WAITING ROOM IN THE EMBASSY OF THE DEAD

And then they were back in the Embassy. Jake couldn't quite believe it was all over.

There was Cora, standing by the glass panel that split the familiar waiting room in two, and on the other side of the glass was Herman Poltago, his feet up on the desk and his sun hat tipped over his eyes. He was fast asleep.

'I suppose we just wait here . . .' Jake began as he walked towards Cora, but he stopped as she turned towards him and he saw the expression on her face.

'What's up, you look like—'

A voice spoke from behind him.

'Like she's seen a ghost?' it said.

Jake spun round. It was the Captain! He was

standing between them and the shimmering doorway to the bridge.

'What I can't understand is how can Jake Green, aka *the Wormling*, be here, in the Embassy of the Dead, if his body is –' he paused to smooth his moustache – 'currently being eliminated by Portentia.'

Jake's blood turned to ice.

The Captain smiled. 'Common sense informs me that an interfering Bodyshifter and known cohort of Amber Chase *must* be involved.' He rolled his eyes. 'I should have realised Eustace would get tied up in this mess. They were very close. It just goes to show, you must be careful who you get involved with in life – and death for that matter. Loyalty can be such a weakness.'

He grinned and moved a step closer to Jake. 'Of course, neither you nor he will survive the elimination of your body, and Amber too won't be alive for much longer. Still, it was a brave effort on all of your parts, I must say.'

Cora snarled. 'I don't know what you're smiling about,' she said angrily. 'It's over. You've *lost*.'

The Captain smiled again. 'I heard! The Authorities are on to me, eh? At this very moment searching the Embassy to find and arrest me? It's all very inconvenient.' He smoothed his moustache. 'And now the demon can't cross the bridge and you've won, correct?'

Jake glanced at Cora. The tone of the Captain's voice didn't seem like someone whose plan had just been foiled. He seemed strangely triumphant.

'Unless of course ... it's here ... *already*?' he said, his eyes shining.

'What do you mean?' asked Jake, a feeling of anxiety growing inside him.

'I only mean to say ... well, what if the demon had *already* crossed, *before* you closed the bridge, say, before you even ... left?'

'But ... but that's not possible!' said Cora. 'Amber knew that it would cross at sunrise. She heard the plans being made. There's no way it could be here ...'

The Captain smiled. 'Really? Are you sure she heard absolutely correctly? Well, you know best. After all ... it's not like you're a mere child dabbling in things you couldn't begin to understand, is it?'

The news that the demon was about to be stopped didn't seem to bother him at all. Jake and Cora exchanged nervous glances.

Maybe it wasn't over?

Something the Captain had said before the Undoer Ceremony stirred somewhere deep within Jake's memory.

Always turn up early for a fight. Especially if it means your enemy are asleep.

Had he tricked them all?

The Captain turned and limped across to the doorway to the bridge that Jake and Zorro had just stepped through, which, as Jake and Cora now saw, was still shimmering there in the corner of the room.

'But you can't!' shouted Jake. 'You can go through the door, but they've shut the bridge! They'll get you at the checkpoint.'

The Captain laughed. 'The Authorities have only closed the bridge *one* way. Nothing can get in, but I can get out! I shall simply merge with the thousands of newly passed currently trudging their miserable way to Deadhaven. But unlike those unfortunate souls, I shall be welcomed by the new rulers of the Afterworld! Anyway, it's been a pleasure . . .' he said, turning to wave at them.

As he did so, Cora growled and leapt at him, swinging her hockey stick furiously.

The Captain bellowed and threw up his hands to deflect the blow. He spun round furiously and tried to grab the stick from her, but she pulled it back, and as the Captain lost his grip, the stick went flying backwards, smashing into the glass partition that separated Jake, Cora and the Captain in the waiting room from the Wight, Herman Poltago. As the stick made impact, a great zigzagging crack spread across the glass. Poltago's eyes opened. He yawned, stood up, and peered at them through the glass. The cracks distorted the slow smile that spread across his face.

He put a finger against the glass and pushed.

For a moment, nothing happened. Then the

whole pane of glass shattered, falling in thousands of splinters on to the floor.

The Captain looked at Poltago, who was smiling strangely. The Wight climbed up on to his desk and began to crawl through the gap where the window once was.

He looked at Jake.

'Eeny . . .'

Then Cora.

'Meeny . . .'

Then Zorro.

'Miney . . .'

Finally he turned to the Captain.

'Mo!'

He stepped between the Captain and the doorway to the bridge.

'Don't even think about it, Poltago . . .' the Captain said, his voice cracking in fear. 'You work for the Embassy now. Your soul-sucking days are behind you.'

'Once a Wight, always a Wight,' said Herman Poltago, as he closed in on the Captain.

The Captain's back was against the wall. There

was no escape. Herman placed his hands on the Captain's shoulders.

'Let go of me . . .' screamed the Captain. 'No—!' His scream died as suddenly as it had begun.

It took approximately five seconds for Poltago to drain his energies. Jake shielded his eyes from the sight of the Captain disappearing. When he looked up, the Captain was no more. Not in the Earthly Plane, the Afterworld, or the Eternal Void. He was gone for ever.

Herman Poltago turned slowly. His eyes settled on first Jake, then Cora, then Zorro. And he smiled.

'Dessert?'

There was a bang and shouting as the door burst open, and Stiffkey and the Ambassador stormed in.

The Ambassador looked at Poltago. The smile fell from the Summoner's face.

'Get back to your desk,' she said. Herman Poltago held up his hands and backed away from the children.

'Hey. I'm a Summoning Wight. It's what I do.' He looked at Jake. 'No offence meant.'

The Ambassador waved her hand – once more Hermann Poltago was safely behind glass.

She frowned at him.

'You appear to have consumed the key witness,' she said with a sigh.

JOINING THE DOTS

'Well, boy, it's been good to see you, but I hope I ain't going to be seeing you again for a while. Look after yourself, boy.' Stiffkey looked across at the Ambassador, who nodded.

'Herman, keep these two company until I return,' said the Ambassador, as she followed Stiffkey to the doorway to the bridge.

Cora clenched her fists. 'But you can't just leave us here!' she said. 'We can help!'

'I think smashing Embassy property and getting our key witness killed is probably enough help for one day, don't you?' said the Ambassador. 'Now if you'll excuse us, we need to get to the checkpoint. We have a demon to detain.'

'But they're not going to find the demon at the bridge!' Jake said.

The Ambassador turned to look at the Junior Undoer. 'And why is that, Wormling?' she said, giving him a withering look. 'Why would the most powerful magic ever created fail to catch this demon crossing?'

Jake swallowed, realising the ramifications of what he was about to say. *'Because the demon is already here!'*

'Did the Captain actually *say* that?' asked the Ambassador.

'Well ... no,' Jake had to admit. But he knew it, he just *knew*.

The Ambassador rolled her eyes and turned back towards the doorway.

'Then we best be following Amber's clues for now, boy,' said Stiffkey, taking his hat in his hands. 'Hopefully they've got the demon at the checkpoint and then we can all be going home and forgetting about this whole nasty business.'

Stiffkey paused there in the doorway for a moment, looking back at Jake. 'This boy ain't

233

got long,' he said to the Ambassador in a quiet voice. 'We need to get him back to his body soon, or . . .'

She nodded. 'I'm confident Eustace will be keeping it alive. He's a skilled Bodyshifter. But for now, frankly,' she continued, 'it's not a priority. Not when a plague demon is at large and twenty-five million lives are at stake. Hopefully we'll be back shortly with good news.'

And with that, they walked through the doorway to the bridge and were gone.

Jake stared after them furiously. 'I know the demon's on the Earthly Plane!' He glared at Cora. 'We *have* to work out where.'

'But it could be anywhere,' she replied, slumping down into the chair by the desk. 'If it's already here, then we're doomed.'

He paced the room, wracking his brains for a clue.

'What if the Captain *was* working ahead of time? Was he just tricking *everybody*? Even the smugglers? Or could "sunrise" have had some other meaning that Amber misunderstood?'

Cora had picked up a copy of **THE BOOK OF THE DEAD** that was on the desk. 'I wonder what **THE BOOK OF THE DEAD** says about plague demons?'

She turned to the section on plague demons and began to read. A moment later she looked up at Jake with wide eyes.

'Listen to this – *On arrival in the Earthly Plane, a host must be found and inhabited, whereupon the micro-demons will be able to take a physical, earthly form. This gestation and hatching process usually takes around six hours.*'

Jake looked at Cora. 'So maybe it wasn't that the demon was *crossing* at sunrise after all ...' he said. 'Maybe it was *hatching* at sunrise!'

'And if the demon was hatching at sunrise,' said Cora, joining up the dots, 'it would have to have come on the first crossing ...'

'At midnight! Which would mean ...'

'It was at the club when we got there! Before we'd even crossed. Just like the Captain said!'

'Of course! That explains it ...' said Jake. Something else had been bothering Jake. He was thinking about the boatman. And his strange illness. And he remembered something else Stiffkey had said.

Only thing makes you sick in the Afterworld is a plague demon . . .

'The boatman was ill because he'd been in contact with the artefact containing the demon!' he spluttered.

And then everything suddenly clicked together, like the pieces of a particularly macabre jigsaw, as he remembered . . . on the floor of the wardrobe . . .

'The suitcase!' he shouted, and Cora's eyes grew wide.

'Of course! With all the jewellery in it! Maybe one of those jewels was the artefact containing the plague demon?'

And as she said it, they knew it must be true. Their faces fell.

'It could be anywhere now,' said Jake, the full gravity of the situation bearing down on him as he slid down the wall on to the floor and held his head in his hands. 'And the Captain is dead, so we can't ask him . . . We're doomed.'

A terrible silence filled the room.

'Hey, kids, don't be down!' said Herman Poltago, breaking the silence. They both looked at him. They had completely forgotten he was there.

Herman smiled. 'The Ambassador will stop the demon, I'm sure of it. It's probably at the checkpoint.'

He took a mint from the tin on his desk.

Cora sighed. 'I thought you might actually have something useful to say then.'

Jake watched as Herman flicked the mint into the air, readying to catch it in his mouth. It spun through the air, catching the light. It reminded Jake of something. Something that had come from the suitcase. Something flicked casually across a room, a reward for loyalty.

Jake gasped. He had been right! Malthus *was* already here. He was in the ring. The ring that Portentia had slipped on to her finger. About six hours ago.

'The ring!' he shouted. 'The Captain gave Portentia a ring from the suitcase . . . She's the host! The demon's in the ring!'

Cora's eyes widened. 'We have to get to her! The demon will be hatching *right now*!'

'Then it's too late. We don't know where she lives. We're miles away from anywhere.'

Cora banged her stick on the floor in anger.

Jake thought for a moment, then smiled. 'Unless ...'

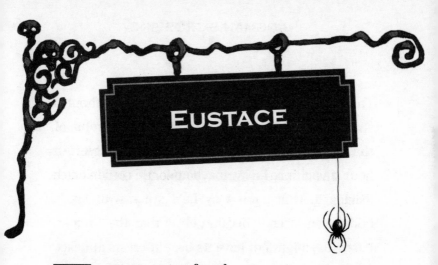

EUSTACE

Eustace was confused.

Not another strange voice disturbing him from his slumber? Who could it be? And where was he anyway?

'Eustace!'

The strange voice was louder now. And harder to ignore. It was coming from behind him.

'Hello? Hello? Eustace . . .'

Eustace sat up slowly and looked around him. Snatches of memory were coming back to him now . . . the club, Portentia putting him to sleep, the boy . . .

The boy whose body he was still inhabiting!

No wonder he felt strange. Eustace had never spent as much as six hours inhabiting a living person before. But he couldn't leave Jake's body.

The amount of time a body would live without a spirit inside it, like the ones left in the cloakroom of the Embassy of the Dead, was unpredictable. An hour if you were lucky, maybe two. He couldn't risk leaving it, which was why he'd stuck with Jake's body even after it became clear that the Undoer, Portentia, might not have its best interests at heart. That and the fact that she'd put him and the body he was inhabiting to sleep with some very powerful (and, he might add, strictly forbidden) Old Magic.

Now he had come to, he found himself on a soft bed that smelt of expensive perfume. He couldn't see it, as Jake's eyes were still sealed shut by the magic, but he could feel it, and smell it, and it was a fragrance Eustace had to begrudgingly admit he approved of.

The tiny voice nagging at him he did *not* approve of, though. Why wouldn't it stop? His head hurt. But wait ... was that the boy's voice? Was he trying to call him? If only he could wake this stupid body from its paralysis, then he might be able to answer it ...

'Eustace, please!'

If *he* was awake, then surely Jake's body must be beginning to wake up too. With a bit of effort, Eustace found he was able to force open Jake's eyelids. This was a good start, though as he couldn't move his head, he could see only ceiling. A nice ceiling. But just a ceiling.

He tried to move his body and Jake's right arm twitched. Eustace tried again. It slowly lifted into the air.

So now he had control of one arm and two eyelids. A slight improvement.

He looked around as much as possible by swivelling his eyeballs. He was indeed in a very nice bedroom. He approvingly noted the Egyptian cotton bedsheets and pushed himself over to his side to look around. No mean feat considering he only had one working arm and was still wearing a backpack.

He smiled. There was an expensive-looking vase of lilies on the bedside table.

'Lilies? How pleasant,' he muttered, realising, given he had just spoken, that the rest of Jake's face must be waking up.

The voice was getting louder now. It seemed to

be coming from behind him. He pushed himself over on to the other side. But still it was coming from behind him! He was about to push himself back to his original position when he realised . . .

It was coming from his backpack.

'Oh, for goodness' sake! Whatever happened to a classic leather briefcase.'

He struggled out of the rucksack and unzipped it with his one good hand and his mouth.

He rummaged inside. A trophy . . . weird. And a small wooden box. The voice seemed to be coming from the box. It was marked with the Embassy logo – a Necrommunicator! Jake's handler must be trying to contact him. He fished it from Jake's bag with Jake's single working hand and pushed open the drawer.

'Hello . . . please answer, Eustace . . .' croaked the squashed and dehydrated dead mouse. The voice was beginning to sound quite desperate. Eustace flicked the switch.

'Helloooo . . .' he replied.

The mouse sat up suddenly. 'Hi! Eustace. Thank goodness. It's Jake. I'm at the Embassy. I need to get there now. Erm ... Do you mind if I take my body back? I think you just need to throw a glass of water or something over my face.'

Eustace sighed with relief. 'Jake, my dear boy. I think I can just about manage that.' He reached out with Jake's good arm to the expensive-looking vase of flowers by his bed. 'In fact, it'd be a pleasure ...'

PORTENTIA

Portentia stood on the balcony of her penthouse apartment, gazing out across the view of the city. A redness burnt the morning sky, the glow from the morning sun as it crept up from the horizon. She fiddled with her ring, feeling the smoothness of the gemstone between her fingers.

The Captain had said he'd be here by sunrise. *Where was he?* She hadn't felt herself all night, for some reason. Maybe she was just tired. I mean, it wasn't like she'd been able to sleep. The Wormling was passed out in her bed. Amber Chase, too, was still unconscious, on the floor of her bathroom. Portentia had managed to help her with a bit of the Old Magic but the Captain would have other plans for her, and there would be nothing she could do about that. Not now.

She took a new pack of cards from the window sill before her, and punctured the plastic wrapping with a fingernail.

How was the Captain going to fix this?

She flipped a card from the deck.

The Sun.

A new beginning.

The Devil.

Something evil was coming.

She frowned at her reflection in the glass wall.

She was looking tired, ill even.

Taking a deep breath, she took another card. And what did the future hold for her?

She looked at it and closed her eyes. Her hand opened, unwilling to accept the card that her fate had dealt. The card fell to the floor, face up.

The Fool.

She knew it now for sure. The Captain had lied to her.

She had been tricked.

She put her hand to her face. A thin line of blood was trickling from her nose.

A ROOM IN THE SKY

Jake's eyes were already open, but the effect of his spirit suddenly leaping from the Embassy of the Dead to a bedroom on the top floor of a skyscraper was like he had blinked and the entire world had moved.

Plus, he was soaking wet and covered in flowers. Jake was back in his body. It felt good.

'Awfully nice to see you again,' said Eustace, toasting him with his ever-present cocktail glass. 'Now you've got your body back, I'll be heading off . . .'

'Wait . . . Where's Portentia? She's wearing a ring containing the plague demon. Any second now it's going to hatch!'

'Jake, dear boy. I have no idea. I've just woken up . . .'

'We *need* to find her.'

'Well, if you must, you must. I might stay in here, though, if it's all the same to you. I'm not really the fighting sort.'

'Fine,' said Jake, and was about to leave when he heard a loud knocking sound coming from the bed.

'Oops, almost forgot,' he said, rummaging in his rucksack and pulling out the trophy. As he flicked the lid closed and open again, Cora came whooshing into the room, looking furiously angry, and with Zorro tucked under one arm.

'Took your time about it!' she said, putting the fox down.

'Sorry,' said Jake. 'Are you ready?'

Cora nodded, and they opened the bedroom door.

On the other side was a larger room, surrounded on all sides by huge floor-to-ceiling windows and a glass sliding door, leading out on to a balcony. And standing in the open doorway, taking in a beautiful, sunny morning, was Portentia.

Jake and Cora looked at each other. 'The sun's

definitely risen then,' whispered Cora. They hadn't been able to tell in the bedroom as the curtains had been drawn, but now it was – quite literally – as clear as day.

Portentia spoke without turning.

'Hello, Wormling,' she said. 'You've woken. And who have you brought with you?'

'Um, this is my friend Cora,' said Jake, unsure what else to say.

Still Portentia didn't turn.

'I'm not sure how you got her into my home, but welcome. Look around you. What do you think of my collection?'

Jake and Cora cast their eyes over the strange objects on display in the room. There were jewellery and artefacts everywhere, strange-looking rocks of the like Jake had never seen, unusual sculptures, including a small stuffed animal that looked suspiciously like a Foreboder and even a huge sword – like a samurai sword – with strange runes carved along its blade enclosed in a glass case on the wall.

But more exciting to Jake than any of these

artefacts was – his mobile phone, resting on a side table. He didn't mention his preference to Portentia.

'Beautiful isn't it: the greatest collection of Afterworld artefacts ever assembled on the Earthly Plane. The picture behind you was painted by Pablo Picasso two months *after* his death . . .'

Jake looked at the painting. To be honest it looked like something *he* could've done. Certainly he wouldn't have risked getting into trouble with the Embassy to put it on his bedroom wall. But this wasn't the time to discuss the finer points of art.

'Listen, the ring . . . You've been tricked . . . It contains a plague demon . . . Take it off, quickly!'

Portentia turned to face Jake. The hand wearing the ring was raised, covering her right cheek. 'I know, I know,' she said with a sad smile on her face. 'I'm afraid you're too late.'

She dropped her hand to her side. Jake and Cora gasped. There was a hole in her face, a hole filled with a seething mass of maggots and winged insects, sticky with mucus.

'My transformation to Malthus has begun,' she

said. Her voice sounded different, as if it had been joined by another, deeper voice. The two voices spoke as one. 'His demon form is merging with my living spirit. His knowledge is merging with my mind. I am him. He is me.'

She took a step towards him.

'Each hatchling moth carries my plague. Once they are airborne, I will be unstoppable. A mere touch will infect the living and they in turn will further spread the plague . . .'

Portentia blinked. A tear ran down her cheek, and she held a hand out towards Jake. For a second her voice returned to normal.

'I never wanted this . . .'

She shook her head.

'I misread the cards. The Captain has played me like a fool. What better place to launch a plague than from the top floor of a skyscraper in the middle of one of the most populous cities on the Earthly Plane . . . This cursed ring . . .'

She reached a hand out to Jake again, and the ring glistened black in the sunlight. He began to move forward to take it. Maybe it wasn't too late to take it off. Destroy it somehow . . .

'No!' shouted Cora.

He looked again at Portentia's hand, ignoring the beautiful gemstone. It was starting to rot and fall away, as the maggots ate away her flesh.

He stepped back. Cora gripped her hockey stick and held it aloft, hanging in the air, ready to strike.

'It's your just deserts,' Cora hissed. 'You shouldn't have been so greedy and betrayed your partner!' She looked around the room. 'Where is she? Where's Amber?'

Portentia pointed to a door, then coughed and stumbled forward, falling to her knees. Her hands pressed flat against the floor.

Jake rushed forward to help her. Maybe he could still take off the ring somehow. He had to try *something.*

He stopped short, recoiling in horror as Portentia's body twisted forwards, disappearing beneath the maggots eating away at her from the inside. In seconds there was nothing left of the human that had once been and instead it was as though the horde of insect life had grouped around her fallen skeleton, crudely mimicking her form. A mass of maggots, chrysalises, and hatchling moths – still wet from the goo from which they had been formed. The only memory of Portentia were the torn shreds of the black dress that hung from this obscene demon.

'Gross!' said Cora.

Jake took a deep breath. He was panicking now. 'Portentia? Can you hear me? We have to get the ring off . . .'

The demon's head looked up, its face a mass of grubs crawling around each other. Then it slowly stood. It was *tall*. Taller now than ever Portentia had been. Ten foot tall at least. And half as wide across.

A puckered hole opened where once a mouth might have been. 'Portentia. Is. Dead,' it said. 'Long. Live. Malthus.'

Not for the first time Jake cursed his stupidity. He'd thought he had more time, he'd thought he'd be able to persuade Portentia to take the ring off. Would that have even worked? It didn't matter now.

Malthus had manifested and his plague moths

were about to hatch.

Jake was too late to save Portentia. He was too late to save the living world.

Cora jumped forward, readying her hockey stick.

'Us Sanderfords don't go down without a fight,' she shouted.

Jake looked around the room in desperation for something he could use to attack the demon. His eyes settled on the sword hanging on the wall and he ran towards it.

'Cora, smash the case!' he said, and for the second time that day, Cora brought shattered glass raining down on them.

Jake gripped the sword by the handle and, raising the heavy weapon clumsily, he ran towards the demon and swung at it with all his strength.

The blade cut through the demon's body. The momentum of Jake's swing caused him to tumble and fall, dropping the sword. It skidded across the floor out of reach.

For a split second, Jake allowed himself to believe that he had slain the demon, but then he turned and looked up at Malthus. The demon hadn't even registered the sword's blow. The crawling grubs had merely parted and then reformed around where the blade had been.

Now it was Cora's turn. She swung wildly at the demon with her hockey stick. But it was similarly futile. The demon didn't even seem to notice.

Cora looked at Jake. 'What do we do now?' she said, and for the first time, Jake heard real fear in her voice.

'I don't know ... Second these moths fly, we're done for ...' He could see them now, amid the mass of maggots, flexing their wings, trying to escape the goo.

'Shut all the windows!' said Jake, running over to the huge sliding glass doors that led out on to the balcony and pulling them closed. 'Maybe we can contain it at least?'

'Listen, Jake ...' said Cora, her voice calm again, the shake completely gone. 'You should go. Me and Zorro are already dead! It can't hurt us,' she said with a sad smile.

'No way, I'm not leaving you. We can beat this!'

But in his heart he didn't believe it. How could they stop something so powerful?

Malthus turned towards them. Jake and Cora backed away from the demon in horror and for some reason Jake found his hand reaching instinctively for the pendant around his neck, as if it might protect him somehow.

As his fingers curled around it, again Jake experienced the strange flash of light and swirling gust of wind, just as he had done in the hollow of the Hangman's tree.

'What was that?' asked Cora looking at him.

'Did you feel it too?' said Jake.

'Jake, the . . . the tooth . . .' said Cora, pointing at it with a shaky hand.

And looking down, Jake could see now that it was glowing, silver-white, like the tip of a scythe.

'What *is* it?' she said.

There was no time to answer. Malthus stepped towards them, arms outstretched. Then it threw back its head and opened its gash for a mouth. 'Long. Live. Pestilence!' it screamed, and the room was filled with a deafening buzz as Malthus exploded into a dark cloud of flying insect life.

Jake didn't have time to think. He just acted on instinct. As the moths swarmed forwards, he ripped the pendant from his neck and slashed at the air in front of him, wielding the tooth like a dagger. He felt it snag on something, then give.

There was a rushing sound. It was the sound of air being sucked fast through a tiny hole. And there it was – between Jake and Cora and the swarm of insects – a small rip in the air. And as they watched, the rip grew and, to their amazement, through it they could see the swirling blackness of the Eternal Void.

It was sucking the insects towards it.

Jake and Cora watched open-mouthed as Malthus and his insects were sucked, limb by limb, moth by moth, into the swirling Void until, almost as fast as it had manifested, the plague demon had completely disappeared, the rip closing itself after it as the last moth vanished.

Jake and Cora looked around in stunned silence. All that was left of Portentia, of Malthus and of the plot to spread a plague across the globe was the shreds of the unfortunate Undoer's tattered dress and, on the floor beside it, a single tarot card. A skeleton dressed in the robes of a priest.

Judgement.

Jake collapsed on to his back, exhausted. He held the tooth up before his eyes. It had torn a hole in the air, a new doorway, straight to the Void.

'What *is* that thing?' asked Cora.

Jake smiled, closing his hands around it. 'I don't know ... but it's mine.'

A moment later there was the sound of the door being kicked open, and Stiffkey and a team of guards came rushing in.

Jake closed his eyes, too tired to have to explain, too tired to do anything but sleep. He heard Stiffkey's voice saying, 'Check the rooms, make sure Amber and Eustace are safe.' Then Jake heard Stiffkey's voice grow softer as he bent down beside him. 'It's all right, boy, it's over. You did it.'

Reluctantly, Jake opened his eyes. He looked at Stiffkey. The old ghost was frowning.

'Old Magic hangs heavy in the air, boy. There

something you want to be telling me about?'

Jake opened his eyes and looked up at the ghostly undertaker. But Stiffkey's eyes weren't on Jake. They were on the tooth, a look of growing concern on his face.

'It's a long story,' said Jake.

'Jake slashed at the air with a tooth he found hidden in the Hangman's tree and it opened up a portal to the Eternal Void and sucked Malthus into it!' said Cora.

Stiffkey raised an eyebrow.

'That's about the size of it I guess,' said Jake, unable to meet the old ghost's eyes.

'Right,' said Stiffkey, 'well that seems like a conversation we'd best be having at the Embassy. I'm sure the Ambassador's going to want to hear about this.'

Jake and Cora groaned.

'But first ... we'd better get you home, Jake, before someone realises you're missing.'

Jake sat up with a start. Sammy's alarm was set for eight a.m. It must be nearly that by now. He had to get back to Sammy's before Sab or Sammy realised he was missing and phoned Jake's home.

'I've gotta go now,' he said, pushing himself up, grabbing his phone from the side table and running into the other room to get his rucksack. 'Otherwise I've got a bigger problem on my hands than the dawning of an Age of Evil: Mum!'

SAMMY'S FLAT

Sab was already sitting at the breakfast table when Jake got in.

'Where have you been?' he said. He looked a bit cross.

'Sorry, I just went for a walk, to get some milk,' said Jake, holding up the pint of milk he'd grabbed on the way back, just in case.

'You look like you've been out all night!' Sab said in an accusatory tone.

'Yeah, no, haha, just didn't sleep that well,' said Jake, rubbing his eyes. When *had* he last slept, come to think of it ... it felt like an age ago.

Sammy wandered into the room drinking a coffee, grabbed something from the kitchen counter, then wandered straight out again.

'You kids better get ready . . .' he shouted from the hallway.

'So, you looking forward to Gamercon today?' asked Sab a bit grumpily. 'Or you gonna be too tired?'

If there was anything Jake needed today, it was to just hang out and play computer games like a normal kid.

'Tired? No way!' he said, putting on a big smile. 'I'll be fine. Can't wait.'

Sab was still looking at him. 'Good. Because it *is my birthday today* in case you haven't forgotten.'

Jake slapped his head. How could he?? That was the whole reason they were there . . . 'Happy birthday!' he said, jumping up to slap Sab on the back. 'Of *course* I haven't forgotten.'

'Yeah right,' said Sab, smiling now. 'Idiot.'

'Yeah right, Precious,' said Cora, appearing suddenly. 'Some friend you are.'

Jake ignored her. He had told her to stay hidden, but she never listened to him so he wasn't sure why he bothered.

'Hey, what's that?' said Sab, reaching for the pendant around Jake's neck.

Jake snatched it back more forcefully than he meant to. The light in the room seemed to flare for a second. 'It's ... it's nothing. Just a necklace,' said Jake.

'Very convincing, Precious,' said Cora. 'Well done.'

Sab's face went pale and his mouth fell open.

Jake looked at him. 'W-what's up?' he asked nervously.

Sab blinked.

'What's up, Sab?' asked Jake again, looking anxiously between Cora and Sab. Sab seemed to be staring right at her.

Sab leant right forward and said urgently, 'Don't turn around ... there is a ... behind you ... a semi-translucent ... a schoolgirl ... *a ghost!* I think. She seems to know us. She said something ...'

Now Jake's mouth fell open. He turned around to look at Cora, who just shrugged.

'Don't ask me, Precious,' she muttered.

Sab's voice lowered to a horrified whisper. 'She called you *Precious* . . .'

'Oh brother,' said Cora.

Jake took a deep breath.

'Sab, there's something I need to tell you . . .'

Will Mabbitt has an overactive imagination. It used to get him in trouble, but now it's his job. His first book, *The Unlikely Adventures of Mabel Jones*, was shortlisted for the Branford Boase Award. He's achieved little of else note, preferring to spend his time loitering in graveyards looking for ideas. He lives with his family on the south coast of England.

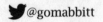 @gomabbitt